'...ty Birmingham
...rent and
...tions,
...ng, do
... Charlie Hill's intelligent
... Things captures their culture with
... arity. His novel charts the years between
... e and the height of the road protests, an age of
... ndulgence, where the partying never ends but
the politics never quite get going. It is, like the suburb itself,
playful, unruly and bursting with generous energy.'

Jim Crace

The Space Between Things

Charlie Hill

Indigo Dreams Publishing

Indigo Dreams Publishing

First published in Great Britain 2010 by:
Indigo Dreams Publishing
132, Hinckley Road
Stoney Stanton
Leicestershire
LE9 4LN

www.indigodreams.co.uk

ISBN 978-1-907401-20-6

British Library Cataloguing in Publication Data. A CIP record for this book can be obtained from the British Library.

Designed and typeset in Goudy Old Style by Indigo Dreams Publishing.

Printed and bound in Great Britain by Imprint Academic, Exeter.

Cover artwork from themightyvern.com adapted by Ronnie Goodyer at Indigo Dreams.

For Joe

Acknowledgements

With thanks to Ruprai Food and Wines for their sustenance and to all of my readers for their advice and support, especially Francis B, Julie, Jacqui, Ann L, Stuart, Laura and Sarah. Thanks to Dangerous Davies for keeping me focussed early doors and to Martin and Dave and Tim for their friendship. Thanks to Ronnie and Dawn for publishing the damn thing. And thanks, of course, to Andrea.

And generally let every student of nature take this as a rule: that whatever his mind seizes and dwells upon with peculiar satisfaction is to be held in suspicion, and that so much the more care is to be taken dealing with such questions to keep the understanding even and clear.

Francis Bacon

Beginning.

There was a woman once, as there always is. I am writing this to try and make sense of her and of our time together. I shall try to be objective even though - as she once said - ours was a time when that didn't seem to matter very much.

The woman's name was Verity, although she didn't like to use it too much in case she frightened people away. It was a difficult name and she thought it was unfashionable and she may have been right. Vee's gone now but she's there in the stillness of the day. She's there in the chatter too, alive even as it deadens my senses. She is the loudest and softest part of the chatter, like the beat in my head and the poetry I once recited and every time I hear her I feel as though I have discovered the great yes all over again and then I feel a terrible pain because there is nothing else to discover and all there can be is loss.

The loss is greatest in the stillness.

~

I met her one day in November 1990. It was a day alright, a day when three and a half years of communal blood-rushes and collective gaps, of self-loving and loathing, of existing, truth-seeking and graft lived in snippets and nearly-times then died, rotted and was spread to the edges of one 24 hours of confused and facile young dreams; a day not fully one thing nor another but one which went hither and thither and swirled in eddies of time and emotion before simply giving up the whooh-whooh piss-taking sheet-white ghost.

Oh, it was a day alright...

1

1. A day.

We were sitting in a group in a campus pub, The Pot of Beer, when we heard that Thatcher had gone. She was in tears, the bitch. Our first thought was 'where's the party?'

The party was in Moseley, two-and-a-half Embassy filter out of town on the number 50 bus. There were no miners in Moseley, never had been. Nor steel workers. There were babyboomer teachers, lawyers and doctors. There were newly-MBA'd consultants in consultancies for people who felt they were out of the consultancy loop. But these people lived in Moseley because they had once grown their hair long and amongst these one-time long-hairs lived their long-haired heirs and now that Thatcher was gone it made sense that the party would be in Moseley.

Besides.

That was one thing you could be sure of. The party was always in Moseley.

We made a few phone calls from the box in the corner of the boozer. Hatched a plan. By the time we left the campus we had been joined by friends leaving lectures or the Triangle Arts Centre. Now we were a dozen strong, maybe more. We walked across town in a long group and our knots tightened as we were stretched by the press of pre-Christmas people. They were shopping, urgently shuffling. The city was grey, the odd mohican or Rasta tam shrill in a muted chorus of concrete and brick. There was a bruising chill in the air, our ear bones throbbed and our faces were hot in the cold but we were laughing as we walked.

We smoked cigarettes excitedly on the top deck of the bus. I sat next to Tom. We worked well together, me and Tom. He dealt a bit of hash and as long as I kept finding him smokers, he kept me in smoke. We talked loudly and people on their way home from work looked at us. We didn't care.

'It's over!'

we wanted to say to them,

'It's the end!'

although they couldn't hope to understand what we were feeling because they weren't like us, young and free and on the charge.

Twenty minutes later we were at Sandra's on the Moseley Road. The party had already started and me and Tom took ourselves off for the tour. Sandra lived in a big Victorian house. It was woodchipped and flaky with thready carpets and fierce heat thrown out of seventies house-brick hearths.

In the downstairs front room, off the hall, there was a brown sofa-bed and what looked like a gas-powered television with plastic wood-effect surround. Someone had pushed them up against a wall to create a dancefloor. A sheet hung up against the window. It had been daubed with swirly patterns in bright acrylic colours and a few anarchist 'A's in black marker pen. On the wall, two posters, Bob Marley with a cone and *Blue Velvet*. In the corner of the room, a bookcase with a tape-deck playing a home-made party mix tape. *No More Heroes, Groove is in the Heart*. Four people were dancing, two were sharing Bonjela on the sofa. Next to the bookcase a boy and girl with dreadlocks were getting lairy. They were apprentice crusties, sweaty and dusty. High on bad cider and talking about the tunes. They changed the tape. Now it was the Dead Kennedys and the crusties started to shout along. The party was a thousand parties in a thousand rented houses but it was also the first of its kind, the first since she'd gone. Tom and I looked on.

There was a geezer sitting next to the couple on the sofa. He was grinning and staring at them. He didn't look like a student. He wore a long-sleeved t-shirt, big jeans, big trainers. Everything he wore looked a couple of sizes too big for him. He looked like he had wandered in, off the street and on the lam. A scally. You didn't get too many of his sort round here. Me and Tom watched as he stood up and launched himself at the crusties, risky degrees from the vertical. He asked them about the tunes. They told him it was punk, 'proper music, angry music' and they were convincing until he asked them what they had to be angry about. 'I wanna dance,' he said, 'have you got any ecs-ta-sy? I wanna nother pill.' Eyebrows raised in Tom's direction. He shrugged, shook his head. No-one in Mose did ecstasy. You couldn't afford that kind of kit on the dole. We left the front room, Tom looking back with interest at the acid house head. He'd never taken ecstasy and couldn't resist the pull of a go-further chemical experience, even vicariously.

In the hall on the way through to the kitchen, two lads were drinking pissy beer and frowning. One of them was dressed in a Redskins t-shirt, jeans that looked like they came from a supermarket, DMs and a small woollen hat. The other looked like a proper straight, only somehow straighter. Old bill shoes. They seemed a bit mardy, SWP-style.

They were talking about 'no real socialist alternative' and the 'American butchers' who wanted to invade Kuwait. Tom called them morons and although his political awareness didn't extend much beyond Timothy Leary, that was fine with me. We askanced and moved on.

- 5 -

In the thin MFI kitchen, a fat Scot was waving a bottle of Thunderbird and minding a plastic bucket full of punch. Someone was chorusing along to *Fight the Power*. Someone else had just thrown up in the sink.

A goth in a purple velvet jacket was crouching next to a kid who was sitting on the floor against the wall. She'd got made-up in the dark, he'd white-ied.
'How do you feel?' said the goth.
'Rough,' he said.
Her eyes widened.
'Are you not feeling good? That's OK, I understand. I'm not feeling very good either.'
She addressed the room. 'Excuse me? Can someone come and give me a hand? Hello? I need some help here. He's having a bad time, he needs to sit up. For god's sake! *Does anyone care what I'm going through?*'

I looked at Tom as he stood there surveying the shambles. He looked, as ever, professorial, mad. Sometimes he knew exactly what I was thinking. What I was thinking was that it was difficult to know who was more deserving of our indifference, the kid who had white-ied or the black-eyed goth. Tom shook his head, drank from his can, sucked on a spliff. I took a pull from a bottle of Tartan Challenge I'd picked up from the side. The scotch hit the bingo. I went upstairs. Upstairs, where the older non-drinkers and wannabe-successes hung out, there was a bedroom full of smoke. True to form, it smelled of nice weed not cheap solids. The room was done out like five years ago. It was painted black and white and there were two full-length mirrors on adjoining walls. Betty Blue was being tortured flouncy-pout style on a poster in the corner, next to the door Joe Pesci looked like a rat. Three punters were skinning up on a cabbagy futon. Two people were standing mockstoned, and, high on the idea, were trying to position themselves so that they could see their reflection through the smoke in both mirrors at once. Trying on different expressions for size.

I laughed, perhaps out loud. Stood there, banjoed and rejoiced, rejoiced in the way of things tonight, round here, in the piss-take, the noise-up and the charge, in the nightmares in the kitchen, the fannies in the hall, the crusty no-marks in the front room and now this mob, faux-smoked-up and precious and behind the scenes, too careful and too calculating and too up themselves to mix it with the hardcore. They'd go far, with their calculations, but who'd want to go with them?

I turned to Tom on my shoulder for some wasted validation but Tom had gone and a woman was there in his place. The woman's head was turned and I could only half see her face. Her hair was tied back. It was simply done. She turned round to me and I saw she was beautiful. It was a beauty that made me think of good and bad, what was right and wrong. I don't know if it was the liquor or the smoke but I felt sick and I was sure she felt the same way.

There was something else too, something that was extraordinary and strange yet comforting in its strangeness. It was as though I knew her and had seen her before, even if I couldn't place where. As though I had looked at her many times in the past. I swallowed through my nausea and then my take on the day was starting again and I found myself somewhere after the end of what had gone before - of everything that had led up to this moment - and before the beginning of whatever was coming next. A hiatus in which there were no questions, or none that mattered, where there was only what happened, passing by breathless and endlessly distracting.

'Hello,' she said, 'you're Arch aren't you?'
'What makes you think that?'
'I've seen you around. You sell draw.'
'What makes you say that?'
'Like I say, I've seen you around.'
'Well I don't. Not really. I just help out friends. Who do you know?'
'Ohh, people. I used to live next door. A couple of years back. I did a few bits and pieces myself then.'
'Yeah? Who do you know?'
'Irish Kev, Jamie...Annie and Mick.'
'OK, OK. And what's your name?'
'Vee. It's short for Verity.'
'That's a posh name.'
'It's an unfashionable name.'
'An unpopular name.'
'An unusual name.'
'I should say. What can I do for you then, Vee?'
'I was wondering if you fancied a smoke?'
'Sure. Back at mine?'
'Where's yours?'
'Sandford Road.'
'Shall we go?' said Vee.

On our way out I found Tom, said my goodbyes. He'd just gubbed a handful of mushrooms. He was talking to the acid house geezer, asking him what was going on in his head. It was two minds, lashed together. It was making no sense. Tom'd be OK. There was nothing his head couldn't take. Me and Vee headed out onto a November street washed with streetlight in a cold light mist. We slipped on wet leaves and Vee grabbed my arm.

'Autumn,' she said. 'Autumn in the city. It's beautiful isn't it?'
'Very poetic.'
'Thank you.'
'Do you like poetry?'
'I do, I do,' she said. 'Poetry talks to me.'
'What does it say?'
'Oh, you know poetry. It's all hints and allusion. You pick at them, follow threads, see where they lead. *Then* you hear what it's saying.'
'Blimey.'
'Thank you.'
'Spring's more my thing,' I said.
'Surely not? Spring's too obvious. All that rising sap? With autumn you have to make a bit of an effort. You know, use your imagination, open your eyes, stop being so passive, so lazy. Throw yourself into the world and its possibilities.'
'Oh, I know all about that. Angelheaded hipsters burning for the ancient heavenly connection to the starry dynamo in the machinery of night.'
'Aha,' she said, 'Alan Ginsberg and his 'Howl.' Do you know, I might have guessed?'
'Don't you like it?'
'I love it, it's amazing. It's just what it's become. That whole Beat vibe's just a bit of an excuse for self-indulgence now, isn't it? It's not really my thing anymore.'
'Well then I'm very sorry,' I said and I was.

We walked away from Moseley, down Church Road and the hill towards the mosques and Balsall Heath. The leaves got thinner and the lampposts further apart. Some of the bulbs needed changing. Vee let go of my arm and I reminded myself it didn't matter.

Just past the corner of Church and Beechwood there was the noise of breaking glass. We turned to see someone land limbs akimbo in the drive of a house. He had come through the front window and was badly cut. There was blood on his head and face. He got up unsteadily and walked out into the road. It was a geezer called Little Bill.

'Alright Tom,' he said. 'Good night for it, ennit?' and carried on.

'Did he call you Tom?' said Vee.
'He did,' I said. 'Only in Moseley eh? I was just wondering why I love this place so much. And there it is.'
'Ye-es,' said Vee and a look slid over her face. I missed where it started, couldn't tell what it passed through along the way. It finished at deadpan, a bad place to finish.
'So, anyway,' she said, 'where were we on this poetic autumnal night? Oh yes. It is good news, isn't it? Thatcher going. But you must have mixed feelings...'
'What do you mean?'
'Well, with you and your howling. She was a bit of a gift wasn't she?'
'Good point. What will I have to howl about?'
'...it's a terrible business...'
'...I might have to stop howling altogether...'
'...shocking behaviour, just shocking...'
'...maybe that'll be where the Spring thing will come in. Maybe I'll branch out into the chortle...'
'Maybe, maybe... but seriously though.'

"Seriously though'? Nah, you're wrong there, Vee. Seriousness finished this afternoon. It's over. Just relax, go with the flow. Hereon in, I do declare, the only way is up, baby.'

'But you do think it's good news?'

'Yeah, I suppose so. Mind you, it is and it isn't. I never liked the woman but the other lot are just the same. They're all the same.'

'Who are?'

'People who stick their beaks into things they know nothing about. People who think they know better than other people about how people should live their lives. Politicians. And they don't know better, you know. In fact, they're all going to shit in a shitcart.'

'Nicely put.'

'Thank you.'

'Where did you hear that?'

'Mate of mine, Numpty Frank. He likes to smoke and put the world to rights. He can have some funny ideas at times right enough, but this one seems reasonable. He said that all bets are off. That all that stuff's finished. Politicians, politics, the political, the lot. It's over.'

'Mmm. But surely that's all about trying to make sense of the world? And you can't just stop that... *can you?*'

'Yeah but the point he was making – and I'm paraphrasing here – is that Nelson's walked and the mullets are playing football in no-man's land and so we've already made sense of the world, politically speaking. Now the gorgon's lost her head as well. So there's no more politics because there's no more political arguments to be had. Us, the Eastern Bloc, the Boers, everyone. We're all human, we all want the same thing, so we might as well stop mithering and just get on with stuff. Try to get by.'

'Quite a lot then.'

'I'm sorry?'

'Numpty Frank had quite a lot to say for himself. So what did he mean by just get on with stuff?'

'Oh, the usual. You know, getting by, doing what you need to do. Reading, shooting the shit, listening to music. Getting off your head. *It's how you walk through the fire*, as Charles Bukowski once said. And what could be more important than that?'

'Hmm. Bukowski is it now. Quelle surprise. And are you sure he meant it like that? Because there's lots more important if you can be bothered with it and it doesn't all involve getting off your head or listening to music. Not all of it has to revolve around you, either. There are other people in the world you know.'

'Yeah, I know but if it's all the same to you I'll stick to my version and sort myself out first. Because if I don't then nobody will and I won't be any use to anyone.'

'Nice work if you can get it.'

'What do you mean? It's not easy you know, this life business.'

'I know, I know. Bless. All that existential trauma? But mark my words, young man - no good will come of this.'

'Who said anything about good?' I said and enjoyed saying it.

We arrived back at home. I shared a small house on Sandford Road with a kid called Jason. Jason wasn't about and I was glad. Jason was from the north. He worked in an office for the council. He was a thin man with angles that didn't add up. Most evenings he went to the pub to drink on his own at the pinball table. Before he left the house, he would sit in front of the 9 o'clock news for half an hour of angular bemusement at the world and tan a four-pack of K cider. There was something about Jason. He was a lovely lad but he wasn't the sort of housemate you brought girls home to meet.

Me and Vee stumbled giggling about the house. We smoked and drank and danced with each other and then I put some music on. Then we were in my room, listening to *African Herbsman* and the Velvets and then we were laughing and pretending to try and keep warm and then before we'd thought any more about it we were fucking and then talking some more and then smoking, laughing and making love until we lay down under a thin duvet as the rain that had begun to fall as we arrived home cleared outside my window and a few dead stars shone through the smudge of the sodium haze and then we slid away together and then we were slipping off together and hiding in the darkness.

~

Then I was overcome by an extraordinary stillness. Nothing mattered, nothing moved. And in the stillness there was a harmony, the sense that everything in my world had a place and was in it, and more, the sense that she felt the same. There was a peace. A goodness. In the dark it felt good.

~

And then it was morning and Vee wasn't there. Vee had gone. Just taken off, left nothing but her rolling-baccy scent on my cotton-bobbly sheets. It was insistent, dirty, beautiful, taunting. I didn't even have her phone number. What was she trying to prove by that?

I sat up in bed and smoked a cigarette. Where had she gone? Why had she gone? It didn't seem fair. I mean we were young and free and we didn't do schnookums or MFI. But still.

I wondered if this was about her chat. Despite her playfulness there had been something in her tone. She had talked as if all that stuff about politics and making sense of the world really mattered. As if throwing yourself into the world and its possibilities was somehow a responsibility. I mean I could think with the best of 'em - I liked to think I was good at thinking - but this was different. With her 'nice work if you can get it', it was as though she had been testing me. Seeing if I passed her peculiar political muster. And if she had, then what did this morning's vanishing act mean? That I didn't measure up? So where did that leave me now? It was a challenge, I'd give it that. But unnecessary too. Particularly on a night like last night, when sex was involved and the rest could have waited.

I didn't like it.

I meant what I had said to Vee. In my book Frank had got it right, we'd already made sense of the world. Whatever anyone used to argue about back in the day it was now about just getting by. Keep it simple, that's what I reckoned. Get through the fire. For Vee, this was evidently a cop-out. For Vee, getting by wasn't good enough. You had to work harder. You had to put the graft in. You had to go and complicate the issue.

By one o'clock Vee was still gone and the day was still a mess. Yampy as fuck. Then Tom was banging on my front door with a couple of cans of six percent. I had just arranged to meet my girlfriend, Ella, for a traditional giro day livener in the Fighting Cocks. Me and Tom walked up the hill to Moseley Village, retracing the steps I had taken with Vee. There were city clouds. They were low and it seemed darker than it had last night. I felt under the weather. I couldn't concentrate. There was too much information to take in, too much from last night to sift and order and understand.

On the way up the road me and Tom had a bit of a spraff. His tale was the usual story about the pursuit of the higher experience and despite myself I was almost absorbed in the usual way. He'd stayed at the party until most people had wendied out. Afterwards, he had gone back with some kids to the part of Kings Heath where the football hoolies lived. He'd been burned, buying a bag of aspirin for a fiver, but there was nothing new about that because he was, in the nicest possible way, a bit of a burnable sort. Listening to Tom's chat helped and so then I was telling him about Vee. About seriousness and politics and 'lots if you can be bothered with it.'

The words were strung out but I needed to say them. I liked talking to Tom about women. Tom knew nothing about women. But then he knew nothing about men either. To Tom, men and women weren't to be known. The feelings, motivations and behaviour of individual people were of little consequence beside the infinite possibilities of the human place in the cosmos. Or so he might have said. Most of the time, Tom humoured me. Sometimes I tried to humour him. That was when I got lost.

'Why did you do it?' he asked, not because he really cared but as a friend which was what I wanted. I couldn't answer him, at least not in the usual way and before I'd had the chance to improvise we met Ella outside the Cocks. Ella was streetwise. We had been seeing each other on and off for about a year and a half. Some days I thought Ella was special.

'Why so glum?' she asked.
'Just thinking,' I said.

Then we were in the pub. It was high-ceilinged, high-Victorian. In the mornings it was half-empty. *Paradise City* was on the jukebox, as usual. Terrible song but great in a sarcastic singalongy Jive Bunny kind of way. The tune soaked into stained upholstery, stained it some more. Last night's happy people were still happy. The Friday hardcore were oiling their joints. Tom knew most of them. Sold to some, bought from others. He stayed for a pint and then trapped. It was his giro day and he had head-space to fill. Me and Ella started conversations which drifted from side-to-side to the floor. I remembered I was going to buy some videos. Ella had just cashed her giro and I tapped her for twenty quid. It was only fair. Whatever happened, however I was going to play it, she had to know it wasn't about her.

We left the pub. It was three in the afternoon and the cloud had lifted and was higher. My head felt a little better with the alcohol but not better enough. I sparked up, unsure what I wanted to do. I knew what would happen. We would go back to mine or hers and have a burn. We would wait for the day to fold and then fold again into the darkness of a night in which I would not feel good.

I realised that during the course of the last few hours I had fallen out of interest with Ella. And with that I realised something else, something that had been dread-inducingly obvious ever since I'd set my old-skool googly eyes on Vee. She had got to me. Quicker than anyone, ever. She was different, implacably different. There was difference in the challenge she presented, her wit.

So what was this about? I was kidding myself if I thought that it was just about politics and the way she made me think, yet it wasn't kid's stuff either, the drink or lust. It didn't feel good like kid's stuff. It felt good and bad and everything in between. It felt like sentience, like too much feeling.

It felt like *love*.

And, to be frank, this wouldn't do. What place did love have when you were young and free and on the charge? Love was for people who were happy to have stopped walking through the fire, who'd given up on reading, shooting the shit, listening to music. I knew people stricken by the thing, good people now saving money and staying in, sometimes even shopping at Sainsbury's. Truth be, I'd been there myself, once. Been burned, you might say. When I was a kid, before I knew any better. Her name was Geraldine and she'd lived up the road and gone to the school next door. We'd loved each other too quickly. At 18 she'd left to go to university in Manchester and I'd hated just as fast. Been left with my defence mechanisms and my hurt. (Was that it? Yeah, that was it. Some things are intractable, live and let live, however you want to play it, whatever gets you by. Look inside, by all means, everyone looks inside. But why *dwell*?)

Either way, I wasn't ready for love, not again, not yet. It wasn't right. I didn't want it. It was time to rationalise my feelings, time to pass over the feeling of dread inevitability, time for my mechanisms to kick in. What was it I'd said to Vee last night? Seriousness is over? Well it was. Yeah. Yeah, that would do for starters. That would do fine.

Then me and Ella were outside Tesco and we bumped into Vee. She was with some fella. They were holding hands. Vee looked amazing. Flushed and bed-headed. I had seen the fella around. He wasn't a geezer. He wore a velvet jacket and carried a satchel. He was one of those privileged bohemian types, desperate to lose all trace of privilege. He was a no-mark. He looked very happy. Contentment surrounded him in a glow. Like he was the lover of a woman he'd spent the night loving.

- 17 -

'Hello Arch,' said Vee. 'Arch, this is Rick, Rick Arch.'

Rick's whole person wafted hello.

'Hello again,' I said. 'So, Rick. What's going on? I don't mean...I mean...I didn't expect to see you... Vee?'
'Arch is a man of the written word,' said Vee. 'The Beats wasn't it? And Charles Bukowski? If I can cast my mind back...'
'Well, you've got to like that poem.'
'Which poem?' asked Rick.
'Arch?' said Ella.
'Oh. Yeah right, Ella, Vee, Vee, Ella, Ella Rick and all that. Look, anyway, it's been great but we've got to make a move,' I said.
'See you then,' said Rick.
'Bye,' said Vee.
Then me and Ella were walking back down the hill. I didn't think Vee had been very fair. Ella asked me for her twenty back. I gave it to her.

'Where did you meet her then?' she asked.
'Last night,' I said.
'*What?* I didn't say 'when' Arch. I'm not an idiot.'
'I mean...at a party. Last night at a party.'
'It's a bit - now what's the word? - *ironical*, isn't it?'
'Ironical?'
'Ironical.'
'Describe ironical,' I said. 'I don't know what you mean by ironical.'
'You wanker. You total wanker. You're both seeing someone, that's ironical. Well, better luck next time.'
'Ella?'
'Fuck off Arch.'

I arrived home. It was mid-afternoon. Jason was in the lounge being rude to a can of K and watching 'It' on video. A clown was dismembering a child. I was suddenly tired.

'Taken a flyer,' said Jason. 'Thought I'd get an early start. It *is* Friday. I tell you what, it's been a hell of a day.'

'Pissy,' I said.

'You what?'

'*Pissy*. It's been a hell of a *pissy* day.'

I went to my room and lay down. I suppose I was waiting for the phone to ring. For Ella maybe or Vee. For the world to come to me.

2. Moseley.

After that day, I didn't see Vee for many a moon. I coped. I was happy not believing in politics and I was happy not believing in love. And if my encounter with Vee had suggested that agnosticism was the more sensible choice, I was happy to immerse myself in the distractions of Moseley to keep me from getting too close to any troublesome realities.

Ah, Moseley. Moseley, Moseley. It's time to tell you a little bit more about Moseley. Moseley was two B&H out of town on the number 50 bus, just past the inner city, just before the burbs. Travelling through, it may not have seemed that Moseley could have provided much in the way of distraction. There was a Tesco, on the road out of town, a baker, two newsagents, a carpet shop, hardware store, fishmongers and deli. There were four pubs and four curry houses. On either side of the main drag, Moseley streets were lined with big old red brick houses. Some of these were rented dishevelled or lived in as squats. The houses were fronted by common or garden gardens full of flowers and flowers gone to seed and weeds that were flowering and flowering weeds. Moseley may once have been the best looking district of south Birmingham, now it was fraying round the edges, an unremarkable-looking place.

But Moseley was precious and special. Moseley wasn't about its location or the way that it looked, Moseley was about attitude. No, that's not quite right. Moseley *was* an attitude. A state of mind.

In the late sixties, the old hippies who owned Moseley houses were young radicals and the place had the political in its petals. Back then, everyone was trying to make sense of the world. There were other people, other places, other ways of doing things. There was even a culture you could counter. They hadn't managed to change much of course, the old boys and girls, but that wasn't the point. They were still there in the pubs and at the end of the long garden parties, reminiscing with avuncular bile about how they'd tried. They spoke of Freak Street, Kathmandu in 1967 and Paris '68, about students behaving as students should, about fancying Bobby Kennedy and aping Dylan and then Haight Ashbury, Greenwich Village, the pill and Vietnam. And sometimes, when it was late in the night and there was nowhere else to go, we listened.

So far, so unhelpful. After all, I was trying to blur the traces of Vee, not have a sense of her political animalism assail my every piss-up and walk in the flowery morn. But then there was our lot. Our Moseley. Our Moseley's attitude was different. Our Moseley had no politics, we'd had what had passed for our politics worn away. Sure, back in the day, those of us who'd been to grammar school had done the anti-status-quo thing. We'd all had friends who'd flirted with CND, sported SWAPO t-shirts or gone to benefit gigs in sticky-floored basements of market-trader boozers. We'd bought tapes of Gil Scott Heron and LKJ, singles by The Redskins. And, of course, we'd watched Ben Elton on Friday Night Live, giving the finger to Thatch. Now she was something wasn't she? The Battle of Traf Square in March last year, giving her a kicking for the poll tax? Some of us had even been there.

But all of that was more about Thatcher than politics. And by the time she'd gone she'd won. They'd won. Worn us all down. There was no politics. No-one had any stomach for them anymore. You could argue all you liked - there was no way of making an impact, because there was no impact to be made. And so although we were young and sussed we were unconvinced too, not much of anything and a little bit for everyone with everything once or twice removed.

In the place of the political, our lot had dissipation. That was something we *had* absorbed from old Moseley, the liberating embrace of the off-your-head. Some people thought that it was an easy option but they were wrong. There was a poetry to getting banjoed. It was an art form. A sacrament. There were books to skim, Burroughs and Ginsberg, Kerouac, Leary, Kesey and Bowles. There were fires to walk through and howling to be done. It didn't matter that it was only the doomed among us who could actually see the flames. That was part of the fun. That was part of our Moseley.

~

The summer following Vee's disappearance, the summer of 1991, I was 21 years old and the sun shone. That summer Moseley, always special and precious, was a cherished illusion, a daydream like youth itself. The gardens of the big houses were in constant bloom. The streets were lined with sycamores and limes, rhododendrons and mountain ash. There were bushes of lavender and rosemary that prickled the scalp with their perfume. There was cherry blossom fairy-tailing the pavements and happy-dusting the roads.

That summer me and Tom complemented each other particularly well. Neither of us was in work or looking and we indulged instead our devotion to the creative indolence of the Village. I hadn't mentioned it to Vee but I wrote the occasional poem myself. Some had even been published, in 'zines. Well, OK then. Printed. Even so, I enjoyed it. And whilst I looked for iambic inspiration amongst the brightly coloured Moseley shoals, Tom was content to drift and dredge for more cosmic fish to fry.

Our days uncurled slowly. In the mornings I'd sit with Tom opposite the tramps who drank apple-free cider and conspired with pigeons on Moseley Village green, a scritty patch of grass by the cast-iron Victorian bogs on the main road out of town. Sometimes Tom would exchange a few words and crack a tin or crash a roll-up. He liked the tramps. Appreciated their fish-hooked faces, their net-curtained eyes.

'At least they've given it a go,' he'd say and I'd try to humour him although the best I could manage was a pissy 'bless 'em.'
'At least they've tried', he'd say and then he would try to convince me that there was something about their attitude, something more real than dismal and when he was in the cider I daresay there was and we'd stay as long as we could. We'd stay until the mad fuckers' Korsakoff violence persuaded even Tom that it could be too early in the morning for head music.

Over long afternoons, we'd take acid and shrooms, watch Koyyanisquatsi on tape. Sometimes we played chess. We'd go visiting, delivering draw. We'd make a dozen drops in a fractal mile, supplying poets and punters in bands, our pockets fat with warm weights. We'd be plied with home-brewed wine and hits from home-made bongs. We'd sit on rugs on bare floors and I'd watch as Tom waited until the puff hit home and then weaved his would-be guru mesh, luring people into hastily constructed mind-traps, spinning punters out with ideas or fruit-loop eschatological conundrums. 'Don't sleep,' he'd suggest, when he was otherwise short of inspiration, 'sleep just blurs the edges of reality'. Punters would look to the side and shake their heads and

I'd love it and wonder what, if anything, these quasi interactions meant to my self-contained friend.

He made other deliveries too, to the bad and the damaged, the variously alive. I heard all about them that summer, Little Bill jumping out of the window in the middle of a session, Baxter cornering some student who was round for a draw and forcing him to drop a tab, Herby trying to mug some geezer by threatening him with a syringe full of bad blood and getting his arm broken for his pains, Robbie stealing lead or hangings or Holy Water from the church on St Mary's Row, Mel doing Scottish Jamie one afternoon on his living room floor with Stu and Carrie watching, laughing, drinking rum and playing gin.

Tom seemed at ease with these sorts. Probably because if he had to be exposed to people, it was in their company alone that he could switch off and concentrate on the business of getting wired. For my part the Bills and Robbies and Mels were fascinating and necessary – part of what made Moseley Mose - but not so vital that my fascination endured beyond these Tom-buffered house-calls. Bits and pieces of people, that was what you needed, not indigestible chunks.

In the early evenings, me and Tom would go for a burn in the private park and watch the sun set over the lake. The park was just off the main drag in Moseley. It was fenced off and padlocked. Every nice house that backed onto it was entitled to a key to the gate. For those in rented rooms there was a long waiting list and you had to pay. The park was an enclave. A safe haven. However on top things got, there was always the park. We would crawl in through a hole in the railings down Nice House Road and sit and get stoned. Look at the greenery, watch the ducks.

'Like boys, lying in the grass or playing cryptic games in the weed-grown park,' said Tom.

'What's that then?'

'Burroughs. 'The Yage Letters'. He's talking about one of the places you go if you take yage. It's a South American plant. You can get it now as DMT. It causes a complete rearrangement of the senses.'

'Sounds a bit tricky. What if they're put back in the wrong places? You might start seeing sounds.'

'Like synesthesia you mean?'

'I might do. Or hearing smells. Or smelling tastes.'

'Or talking shite.'

'Ah Tom, it's nice to see you haven't completely lost touch with the corporeal.'

'Moron,' said Tom.

And then at night we went to the pub. Moseley had three pubs worthy of the name, the Holy Trinity of the Prince, the Cocks and the Traf. The Prince of Wales was an old Moseley boozer, strictly pickled eggs and dommies in the snug, Sunday mornings with the sun coming through stained glass windows and catching the blue in the smoke. In the back room there was a juke-box that was so quiet that nobody bothered with it. In the bar there were pony tailed ex-Freak Brothers, social workers and teachers, the occasional Irish face. The Prince was my kind of boozer. Perhaps surprisingly, Tom was a fan too. He always said it was the only pub in which he could hear himself think. With Tom, you were never too sure if that was a good idea or not.

Moseley faces preferred The Fighting Cocks, a hundred yards along the main drag out of town. The Cocks was a listed coaching house, a shambling place with a legendary lights-camera-action vibe that sucked in bright young things like soon-to-be legless moths. The Cocks attracted musicians and groupies and posers dressed in Cuban heels with knitted string vests or nylon shirts unbuttoned to the waist. On an average Saturday you could see five Keith Richards, four Lennie Kravitzs, three Chrissie Hinds, two Morrisseys and any number of hippyshit lead singers from All About Eve. It was balls deep fanny high in fiercely burning beauty, with kids who were strutty, slouchy, edgy, pouty, narkylouche. The Cocks had every rite of passage you'd hoped you'd avoided but weren't too sure you could avoid in the future; the gauche were slapped for spilling pints, the nervous discarded for passing poor patter. It was the sort of place where you saw someone you knew, and if you were with people and they were with people, you could leave it at that, you could settle for seen. At weekends the place was uncontainable. Punters sat or stood on the narrow pavement outside and spilled into the road, a bustle of hustle and threads. On a good night, the Cocks was more than fun. On a good night it was like fucking on a bouncy castle at the edge of the world.

Around the corner from the Prince and Cocks was the Trafalgar. Everyone who could hack it tried to finish their night in the Traf. This was a different prospect. The Traf was the place you came to for unidentifiable pills. It was a pub for people who thought that Moseley was too soft to be part of and too much of an easy mark to leave alone. A queue of Rastas and homies stood outside the door, offering black hash or weed. It stretched almost to the three-man part-time cop shop down the road and the dealers were often looked at, sternly, by hapless old bill. Armed robbers worked the bar in the Traf and it all got a bit Wild West at times. I'd seen people copping barstools and pool cues, once even an axe. New Age Travellers drank in there, selling go-faster powder from the pool-room in the back where everyone seemed happy going slow and the tunes were old skool, Althea and

Donna, Peter Tosh and Toots and the Maytals. The travellers visited at summer weekends or wintered in old army trucks and ambulances parked up in the alleyways of Anderton Park Road. Some of them had done time. Some of them were on serious drugs. They had silly names, like Smurf or Munch or Mickey the Sleeves. On the quiet I marvelled at the freedom of these raggedy-assed boys and girls and I marvelled at the exotic danger in which they couched their tales of trouble on site and the rainbow-tinted shitstorm that was their oh-so-real life.

And then there were the parties. Wherever you were at the end of the night, if you hadn't heard the word about a party, you would just walk the streets, listening for the music, looking for the lights. Getting in was never a problem, although when I was out with Tom and we chanced on an upmarket affair, we tended to let me give it the chat on the door. Tom looked too bohemian for bohemes and even people who wanted to lose all traces of privilege didn't want all traces of privilege nicked.

Occasionally, you'd be knocked back. This wasn't a problem. There'd be another party around the corner. There were parties everywhere. There were house parties, park parties, garden parties. There were impromptu parties, parties weeks in the making, non-starter parties. There were squat parties where the electric would go off and you'd crawl through glass to get to the door, student parties where kids would confuse deep and desirable with depressive and dull, folk jam parties and punk parties, parties where people listened to Betty Boo or Sham 69 or Burning Spear or The Stone Roses or the B52's or The Violent Femmes, parties where people would smoke themselves to sleep or drink themselves sober in the company of jugglers and strummers and wankers and drummers and punters shambolic as coots, parties where you'd talk to upper-class rappers and atonal singers, where you'd swap class chat with a scutter or lay bong tips on a deb and none of it would matter because that was the beautiful pointlessness of it, the distraction of the Moseley party and of dissipation on the dole.

And all the time, amongst the dissolute nonsense and dilettante shite, there were mini-truths pitty-patted between us. Tom was seriously animated by this chat, bless him, but I luxuriated in the inconsequentiality of it all.

How did it all fit together?
we asked ourselves,
where did we come from?
and
why were we doing what we were doing?

and the answers we came up with may have helped us make a little bit more sense of things if I'd cared to think about them but although I went along with the chat because it passed the time in a Moseley kind of way I didn't care, not really, because as long as there was getting hammered and daubing the odd poetic note-to-self none of it needed to make any sense. This would get me by just fine. The rest could look after itself.

And then, maybe a year after I had met Vee, Tom asked me if I still thought about 'that woman' and this was a surprise, partly because he was asking.

And partly because I did.

3. Moseley sex.

It wasn't as if I hadn't made the effort, mind. In amongst the down-to-business highs and recreational sobriety, there had been moments of rational consideration, moments when I'd tried to lose Vee's scent through more practical means.

I slept with other women. It didn't work. It's a silly business, sex in Moseley. All share and share alike. You're only ever one fuck from an acquaintance, two from a sometime friend. The only person I knew who wasn't at it like a rabbit or a rabbit's bit of fluff was Tom. He just wasn't interested. And by the end of '91 I thought he may have had a point.

Because the desperately funny thing was, every time I had sex that year it was Vee who came to me when I woke up and Vee who stayed with me until the next time.

4. Housemates.

In February 1992, I moved into a shared flat above the disused butchers in a row of shops in the centre of The Village. I'd seen the card in the window of the newsagents. 'Housing Benefit Accepted', it said and true enough the floor in the kitchen shook and the place should have been condemned.

There were three of us officially sharing, me, Mike and Stripe. We'd come together in the usual Moseley style. One part unpaid rents, one part friend of friend of friend, one part indeterminate luck. My room overlooked the Fighting Cocks, Stripe was next door and Mike was on the top floor. Tom, who was couch-surfing again having blown one rent-cheque too many on the pursuit of sock-rotting acid and asexual women, had permanent dibs on the spare room.

Stripe had not long moved up to Birmingham from Brighton. He was one of a new type who'd been spotted of late in the corners of the parties and pubs of Moseley. He wore the regulation para boots and combats of a crusty but his dreadlocks were short and neat and he wasn't pointless enough to be the genuine article.

Stripe was a vegan and you got the feeling that he thought Moseley had gone soft, was an easy mark. All those vegetarian part-timers cluttering up the place. Despite the enormous amount of weed he smoked Stripe was a doer. He was always doing something. On Tuesdays it was kick-boxing in Digbeth, on Thursdays rock climbing at the indoor wall on Aston campus. At weekends, he'd leave Brum to go back down to Brighton or London. In everything I saw of him around the house, whether he was stomping about or skinning up or smoking a bifter, Stripe was deliberate, serious.

Not in a good way, either. He was a miserable sort, cloudy of brow and matt-look of eye and he carried considerably more menace than your average crusty. Smiley Rob - who'd known Stripe down in Brighton - told me that he'd only come up here because he'd 'done enough damage' down there. I didn't ask what this damage was. That wasn't the Moseley way. Even so, I decided to keep my distance.

At the beginning of April, Tom gave up all pretence of looking for somewhere else to live and moved his stuff in, three Kwik Save carrier bags and a pack of tarot cards. That afternoon, keen to see what they would make of each other, I formally introduced him to Stripe and left them to it while I went to the laundrette.

In the Traf later that evening, Tom said:
'There's something about him I don't like. There's a certain kind of certainty about him. He thinks he's got answers somewhere, I'm sure of it. I don't trust him. He has the conviction of the dim.'
'But what is he convicted about?'
'I don't know. And I'm not too sure that he does either.'
'I know what you mean,' I said, 'there's definitely something missing. And all that running around he does. He's got far too much energy if you ask me. He's a bit like a more sinister version of Kenny Loggins, on the quiet.'
'*What?*'
'Kenny Loggins. You know, Footloose. And he's gonna shake up this *town*.'

'I don't know what you're talking about,' said Tom. 'And for fuck's sake, Arch, if you are going to talk to me, use fucking English will you?'

Tom could get like this. Even on the infrequent occasions he cared to absorb titbits of mainstream culture he was frustrated with what it offered. I took his point but then it could be handy, as shorthand, at times.

If I had early confidence in Tom's antipathy towards Stripe, I was forgetting the power of The Session. About a week after Tom moved in, I was sitting in our living room when he materialised on the end of the sofa. He looked unhealthy, insubstantial, like a jowly wraith.

'Long time geez,' I said.

'Yes,' said Tom, 'I've been out with Stripe. He's got some new weed, something called super-skunk. It's got higher levels of THC than your usual pressed grass. I haven't seen it before.'

'Uh-huh. Good time?'

'Yes, yes it was. I took him over the private park. It was quite...*trippy*, you know? He was all for building a little fire. I've always wanted to know where people like that go when they trip...'

As an endorsement I thought this was somewhat double-edged. Still, in his capacity as supplier of Tom's cosmic blag de nos jours, Stripe was suddenly flavour of the month. Or, more accurately, the offer of the week.

If Stripe fitted in, somehow, Mike was a different bag of maybes altogether. Because everyone in Moseley tried so hard not to be a type most nearly everyone was. Mike though, seemed less of a type than a gap between types. He seemed to have no distinguishing features, could lay claim to nothing as substantial as style. His face was nearly interesting, almost dull. He may have been of mixed-race, sometime back in the day, but a mix of what was anyone's guess. He dressed conservatively, if that isn't too pejorative a description. In terms of personality, he didn't even seem to have Moseley as a default setting. Certainly none of us saw him drink and he didn't smoke either, except for a very occasional toke on a bifter when he was playing Tetris on his Nintendo. Mike gave the impression that if an activity presented itself that didn't involve sitting around, reading magazines, playing computer games or watching television, he wouldn't give it boot room.

Other than to sign on or collect his dole Mike left the house just once a week in the first three months he lived there and on each occasion it was to go to the flicks. Eventually my frustration at his ever-presence on our sofa outweighed my respect for his refusal to allow himself to be embarrassed into leaving the front room. I decided to have a word. To goad the boy into some declaration of intent.

'Morning geez,' I said. 'Fancy a smoke?'
'No ta,' he gestured with his joystick, 'I've got a can of Coke on the go.'
'OK... Listen, Mike? Do you mind if I ask you something? It's just... I mean we were wondering, that is, me and Tom were wondering, what is it that you do? I mean what do you do? I mean, don't get me wrong, I don't mean you have to do something...it's just that we've never seen you do *anything*.'
'What do you mean?'
'Well, you know. You seem to spend all your time in here. In front of the TV screen. Don't you ever get bored?'
'Hmm. Let's see. No.'

'But you never *do* anything.'

'Whereas *you*, of course…'

'No, of course, no offence. It's just that, you know, I like *stuff*. I like getting off me head and listening to music and going out. Giving it some chat. And, and reading books. Do you listen to music? Do you even read books? I've never seen you read a book.'

Mike stopped his game and looked at me as though I had fallen into a carefully constructed trap. He gestured at the usual scatter of magazines on the seat next to him:

'Why read books when you can read about reading books?' he said. 'It's a lot quicker. I tell you what I *do*, Mister Off-yer-ead, I absorb information, that's what I *do*. I watch and learn. And you mark my words Arch, information is power. Oh yes. You might not see me exercising it, this power, but I know things Arch, I have the information. And the information? *Eees power!*'

I looked at the magazines. I could see a copy of Empire, the NME, Viz and an old Fortean Times. Either Mike knew something I didn't or he was an idiot. Or worse, both.

I still hadn't made up my mind which it was when, the next day, a punter called Tony came round to buy some weed from Tom. Tony was in his thirties and he had the uncomplicated face of a children's pastry chef. He lived with his parents and he inspired much thankfuckfulness in everyone he met - principally for the fact that they weren't Tony - but his enthusiasm for the creatively edgy was undeniably pure Mose. If everyone in the Village was drawing cartoons or playing the guitar, making short films or wringing out novels, Tony had the generous soul of a poet. Literally. Each time I saw him, he would present me with a handwritten verse or two, mumbling modestly about 'something I'm working on' as if he'd been sweating o'er literary endeavours deep into long dark nights of his soul. The difficulty being that in each case he had merely transcribed verses from Moseley-amenable sorts and tried to pass them off as his own. Sometimes I'd spot these appropriations, more often I'd relay what I could remember to Tom and he'd nail their actual provenance. Ferlinghetti cropped up once or twice, Kerouac put in a badly disguised appearance and on one particularly memorable occasion, the boy revealed himself as a word-for-word reincarnation of William Carlos Williams.

What Tony didn't seem to realise was that if everything he presented as his own work had actually corkscrewed from his imagination then he was a bone fide nutter. Even so, it was touching, in a way, this commitment of his to bringing the old firewalkers to a new generation of dilettante wannabes. But not so touching that me and Tom didn't rip the piss out of the boy every time he tried it on. This afternoon was no different. As he left he presented me with the first verse from a poem he was working on about 'how everyone's fucked, man, just going through the motions,' which turned out to be, on closer examination, from the fourth verse of The Waste Land.

'Jesus, that's sad,' I said and Tom agreed, and we both thought that on this occasion Tony may have taken things too far. But Mike was of a different opinion.
'What's sad?' he said, looking up from a copy of i-D, suddenly animated. 'What are you saying? This 'geezer' has copied out a bit of a poem and is trying to pass it off as his own? That's priceless! Absolutely priceless! What a genius!'
'What do you mean?' I said.

'Well he's reinventing himself as someone else, isn't he? Like Madonna and that Vogue. She went all Forties in that. *Vogue, vogue.* From that Dick Tracey film? *C'mon, vogue.* Who'd have thought it? He is the Moseley Madonna! The Moseley Madonna! Oh yes!'

'Yeah, but who cares about Madonna?' I said. 'Madonna's desperate, she's just flogging a dead one. She's only trying to act because she's had her time as a 'singer'. It's come to something if we've got to hold up Madonna as some kind of cultural role model. And anyway, I don't care if Tony is trying to be someone else - and, let's face it, who can blame him - if he's trying to pass off someone else's poetry as his own, he's taking the piss.'

'But that's what everybody's doing now! Nobody writes their own stuff anymore! It's all cover versions! Look at Robson and Jerome! Whitney Houston! The Pet Shop Boys!'

'The Pet Shop Boys? They write their own stuff don't they?"

'Oh yeah? What about 'Where The Streets Have No Name'? It's all about taking stuff that's already there and rehashing it. Look at T2 and Child's Play 3 and, and, let's see, Highlander 2. And Lethal Weapon 2. *And Star Trek 6!* I mean, for fuck's sake! *Star Trek 6!* If you're going to try something new, it's got to be rehashable. You've got to be able to rehash it, man. Look at that geezer with the shark. You know, last year. Damien Heist. He's going to be able to churn that sort of stuff out for as long as he wants! Maybe he'll do a giant squid next. Or a koi carp. It's the franchise, see. *The franchise.* Maybe this Tony geezer's got the poetry franchise! Either way, anybody that does that and gets away with it is a genius. Think about it! There's a never-ending supply of material! It's genius I tells you!'

Since he had moved into the house, Tom had not deigned to acknowledge Mike's existence. Now, with his unerring feeling for social interaction, he judged the time was right for an opening gambit.

'Moron', he deadpanned

and I turned to see him leaving the room in disgust.

For all his faults, I thought Tom was getting a bit unnecessarily humpty with Mike. He was of the opinion that Mike was a bad human because he was 'a voyeur - and a fucking short-sighted one at that'. I knew that Tom wore his erudition heavily - like an army surplus coat in June - and that his pursuit of the higher human experience made him a little inhuman at times, but even so I found his judgement harsh. It was only because he was my best friend that I was prepared to concede he may have had a point. To his street credit, Mike ignored Tom's mutterings. I liked him for that. I also liked the way in which he continually got to Stripe, who had, in the presence of Mike at least, begun to demonstrate the temper of a very angry man.

'Don't give me that technology shit', he ranted one day, incredulous.

Mike had been reading about 'teleworking' - working from the comfort of your own home - and had suggested to me the idea of 'telescratching', whereby you signed-on from your sofa. Then he'd made the mistake of mentioning some cockamamie scheme for a world-wide super computer network he'd read about. Stripe was having none of it.

'It's only idiots who buy into this whole 'progress' thing. It's progress's got us into this mess in the first place. What about the hole in the ozone layer? What about global warming? That's progress for you.'

'What about them?' said Mike. 'While we're at it, that's something I'm not too sure about. Have we got a hole in the ozone layer? Or is the ozone layer too thick? I mean which is it?

It's like that acid rain! When did that stop falling? Sort it out will ya!'

'Tosser,' spat Stripe, 'yeah? Fucking tosser,' and he turned to leave the room in disgust.

On the way out he seemed to think twice, three times. And stopped. He picked up a beaten copper ashtray from our glass-topped coffee table, hefted it to gauge its weight.

'Stripe...?' I said and watched alarmed as he took a step towards the blinking Mike, made as if to brain him, *'Jesus!'*

Stripe paused, the ashtray raised. Flicked it against the wall, in a flat arc of butts and black match stumps. He turned on his para-boot heel and slammed the door.

'No need geez,' said Mike, 'no need', and I had to concur.

I mean I knew Mike was winging it alright, albeit from the recumbent. There was something peristalsis-like about his journey through the pop-loops of TV, fashion, films, the first and last of the news, as they tightened behind him every 24 hours and he was squeezed onto the couch in a lump. But even so, he wasn't causing anyone any grief. He signed on like a good 'un, scammed the housing benny like a no-frills pro. Didn't interfere with the business of draw, didn't pretend to know more than he did. And I had to admit that this leant his vacuousness an honesty that I looked forward to during the course of every third Tommy-sesh or so.

There was another thing. With Mike you were never sure whether or not he knew more than he let on and was having a royal one at your expense. With Stripe it was sure as eggs that he didn't and wasn't. I still wasn't too sure where he was coming from but as far as I was concerned he could fuck off back there.

I'd take Mike's piss-taking over his earnest idiot anger and fancy weed any day. What exactly did he have to be angry about anyway?

One afternoon, we were given a clue. While me and Tom were having a burn and Mike was sat improving his Mario score, Stripe brought round a woman. She looked like an old-skool hippyshit nonsense merchant. She had curls that danced indecorously. In one eye a hey-nonny, the other a nonny-no. And something else I recognised too, even if I couldn't quite place it.

'Alright Arch, Tom mate,' said Stripe. 'Mike. This is Sorrell, a friend of mine.'
'Hey guys, Tom,' said Sorrell, 'how're you doing, yeah? I'm up from Brighton for a couple of weeks, yeah, to raise some awareness for Earth First!'
'Earth First?' I said. 'Is that like Friends of the Earth?'
'Not really. They're all talk, we're more action. We're trying to stop what we're doing to the planet in the name of progress. It's an organic thing, yeah? It springs up, comes from nowhere. We not paying enough attention to our heritage. Sometimes it's like, we're not going to be happy until we've tarmac-ed the whole flipping country, yeah?'
'I know what you mean,' said Tom.
'I blame cars,' said Mike, 'cars are bad. And there are a lot of them about.'
'Building on ley lines, that's just fucked,' said Tom.
'And roads. Roads can be good,' said Mike, 'but only sometimes.'
'Did you know that there is a ley line that goes through Machu Picchu, Easter Island and Perseopolis?' said Tom.
'Yeah?' said Sorrell.
'Can you drive along it?' said Mike.
'Go on then,' said Stripe, 'why don't you just take the piss?'

'No, seriously geez,' said Tom.

'I didn't mean...' said Stripe.

'Because if you read...' said Tom.

'This ley line,' said Mike. 'Can you see it from the road?'

'Tosser,' said Stripe.

'Moron,' said Tom.

'Yeah?' said Sorrell. 'Anyway, we've come up to Birmingham to try and get some people together who feel the same way and I might be coming up again. And this is it, listen guys, do you mind if I crash here sometimes, yeah?'

And so then we were five.

5. Sorrell and Tom.

Stripe and Sorrell enjoyed a typically easy-going Moseley relationship. They saw each other about three times a week and like many Moseleyites, they were none-too-keen on any boyfriend and girlfriend stuff that could have gotten in the way of either the sex or their time apart.

At weekends, in the absence of Stripe - and despite her talk of Green activism - Sorrell seemed content to chill out and absorb Moseley as if to the special and precious born. She'd picked a good time to become acquainted with the place. It was a happy spring that year, Moseley biding its eternal in white blossom and naive greens under the laissez-faire wash of a lemon sun. On the occasions we got together, me and Tom spent fewer afternoons visiting people or evenings in the pub and more time in the private park, impressing criss-cross grass-stalks on elbows and arms, staring languorously stoned at ducks.

Sorrell added a new dimension to our sessions. Or rather a very old one. She was a very fanciable if barely tolerable girl, with thoughts that leapt like jumping sunshine and whether it was her endearing scattiness or calculated battiness, Tom was smitten from her very first 'yeah'.

I was surprised at this. And initially, I was concerned. Tom was vulnerable. His intolerance of humanity wasn't based on a particularly acute understanding of the object of his disinterest. To Tom, people were like ideas, heart-free and bloodless. Because of this I'd always looked out for him whenever he encountered people, in the way you would a child playing near a busy road. Just in case. He didn't know that people could be complicated. People could be dangerous. People could run you over.

But Tom had also pissed me off, as was his infuriatingly insensitive wont. For a misanthrope and friend his head had been far too easily turned by Stripe's largesse with the turbo-bifter. There had been too many recent occasions where he'd cashed his giro and disappeared, only to reappear three days later, spaced-out and with tales of how he'd jumped to conclusions about Stripe that first night and underestimated Stripe and thought that Stripe had some interesting ideas about crop circles or some such nonsense. He'd stopped giving me weed too, saying by way of explanation that I 'should get hold of some of that skunk' that Stripe sold because 'it takes you places'. 'If you try to hitch a lift on that African you're smoking,' he continued, 'it won't get you further than Cannon Hill Park', an observation that wound me tighter even as it advertised the limitations of his commercial nous.

So that was it. I decided that if that was the way he was going to play it, he was on his own when it came to his interpersonal stumblings. It was time the chaperoning stopped.

At first it was uncomplicated stuff. Soon after Sorrell had moved in, Tom raised the subject of what I thought she was doing with Stripe.
'You tell me,' I said. 'You know him better than I do.'
'Yeah, but they don't seem very *compatible*.'
'Well he's no comedy joker, I'll give you that. And he seems very quiet, when he's not shouting. But then maybe he's got a hidden approachable side. Or',
I suggested,
'an enormous cock...'

and I was happy to see him wince.

Matters quickly got more complicated. Sorrell was one of these unfathomable people for whom no detail of their life was too trivial or personal to share with other people. Even other people who - in the normal scheme of things - might be considered too uninterested to give a fuck. In the park she described her relationship in terms of her yin yang and Stripe's yang yin.

'But why is he so angry?' I asked. 'What does he have to be so angry about?'
Sorrell giggled.
'Oh he's a Taurus, yeah? Some people are just born angry. It's ok. I mean sometimes he can be a bit...*violent*, yeah?'
She giggled again.
'But he's alright with you?' Tom said, shocked. 'I mean he's not *violent* with you?'
'Sometimes', said Sorrell and then under her voice, 'if I'm lucky' and she giggled once more and before I could stop myself I blushed for Tom. But then I remembered that he didn't understand and it was then that I felt guilty, at least for a moment that passed.

There was jealousy too.

Sorrell liked to giggle and she liked to talk. Fuck, did she like to talk. After just one night in the park we had learned that she had always had a spiritual side and that she was a Virgo and a free spirit and that she had once gone to sleep with a Mexican Dream Catcher above her head and almost had a nightmare but not quite. She told us that she couldn't wait for summer and the beginning of the annual free festivals, parties all over the country where people made music and showed respect for the land and how to communicate with the spirits of our pagan past. She told us how it was her dream to live on the road and be part of 'a tradition that goes back hundreds, yeah, probably thousands of years. You pitch up, sort out the land, put some music on, people come and party, everyone has a good time and then you pack up and go elsewhere.' She told us about how, the previous summer, she'd taken lots of mushrooms and danced naked around a fire at something called the Forest Fayre. I asked if she'd seen any sprites or wood nymphs or fauns. She giggled and punched me lightly on the arm. Tom sat there looking straight ahead. She told us that she had met the Earth Firsters at a free festival in Wales and they'd explained to her that we were taking our environment for granted and if we wanted to dance naked around fires we'd have to try and burn less wood otherwise soon there wouldn't be any wood to make fires with in the first place, I'm paraphrasing here.

It was at another party in the sticks that she'd met Stripe. She remembered tents decorated with Wiccan sculptures and loud 'dance music.' I called her a 'soil-fetishist' - which wasn't funny but raised another giggle - and asked if the 'dance music' was being played by goblins or elves or giants. By this point, my lack of expert knowledge of the inhabitants of Narnia was beginning to show but Sorrell demonstrated her generosity of spirit by giggling again and hitting me a little bit harder, while Tom looked off into the bushes.

He needn't have worried. Sorrell was yeahing up the wrong tree. Despite my penchant for the odd party, her interminable dribbling made me more likely to go and listen to some Henry Rollins than join her on the Yellow Brick Road. The situation didn't improve. She told us we should hold a Beltane party, to celebrate the spring solstice, that May, in our flat, with indoor fireworks, carefully contained, yeah, and everyone should take microdots and play the fiddle or bongos. I demurred. It was not a convincing pitch. Yet as she talked, Tom listened. And then he talked back.

I knew that when Tom was away with the puff he liked nothing more than an extended riff. He'd use the writers of the Moseley canon as stepping stones and then take the next step into air, confident that some informed idea of tangible indistinction would come to him and he'd rise and fly. These ideas were often poor. I'd always known that Tom chugged great drafts of rubbish books. Everyone who knew him knew that. It was all part of his insatiable quest for answers to the inexplicable. Until now however, I'd not realised just how voracious his appetite for bullshit was.

In the park that first night, in an attempt to empathetically out-cosmic Sorrell, Tom sat on the grass and married his two passions. He spoke in the manner of an Icke-like Godhead as I counted long seconds and suffered Eric Von Dannekin, Aleister Crowley and some Indiana Jones nonsense about Jesus's great grandson being alive and well and living it up in the Dordogne. I mean fair play to the boy, he knew his stuff, but at times he seemed only one step away from Nostrafuckingdamus. He got arsey too, had a pop about closed minds and lack of credulity.
'What do you know?' he said. 'What do you think you know?'
And I said,
smarter than a rat,
'Enough to know that all I know is all I need to know.'
and Sorrell said 'Oooh, you're such a cynic, Arch.'
and Tom turned to me with an adolescent narrowing of his eyes.

~

Once they played pattacake. We were sitting in our front room, having a burn. It was pissing down the heavens. The room was gloomy, it was a long afternoon. Sorrell said 'come on Tom, it's fun' and Tom looked wide-eyed like a boy. I watched as they kneeled, facing each other, him supplicant and attentive. As she pressed her thin palms against his, his fingers brushing hers like lips. As she giggled and squealed at their fumblings and misses. As she began rhyming, and they found a rhythm and each time they touched she held the touch longer, with Tom hooked and Tom lost and Tom longing.

Afterwards he offered to rustle the three of us up some food. Half an hour later he presented us each with a bowl of Smash. On top, tinned sardines and a bloody mess of ketchup.

'Do you eat fish then?' I said to Sorrell, when Tom had gone back to the kitchen.

'Sometimes,' said Sorrell. 'When Stripe's not around, yeah? I do a lot of things when Stripe's not around.'

'Yeah, yeah I know. You're a free spirit.'

'Whatever makes you happy Arch, yeah? And what's wrong with that? Don't try and tell me you're any different. You get what you can, you know that. I've seen you with your women, yeah, women here and women there, I've heard the things you say to some of them and the things you say to the others. Deep down Arch, we're both the same, there's no point trying to deny it. You're not kidding anyone. Be yourself, yeah? Just be yourself. What's wrong with that?'

'No, no, there's nothing wrong with that. Nothing I suppose. OK, yes, you're right.'

Tom came back in with his bowl.

'Look, Tom yeah,' said Sorrell, 'I'm ever so sorry but I don't eat fish.'

and even as I disliked myself I couldn't help worrying about Tom even more.

6. Mechanical failure.

The postcard arrived in an envelope addressed to Sandra. She had been friends with Sandra you see, since they'd lived next door to each other. Close friends, closer than I ever knew. Sandra had resealed the envelope and passed it on to Rasta Darren in Nastysave, he'd seen Screenprinter Lou in the Traf and I'd picked it up from her the next day when I'd dropped round for an afternoon showing of Angel Heart.

The postcard was from Vee.

Vee had written to me!

Jesus.

I took a deep breath. The postcard was from a place called Split. On the front was a photograph of somewhere called Diocletian's Palace. I'd heard of Split but I wasn't interested in its ruined palaces, not before I had her words. I was shaking and my breath shortened as I read, the postcard lit by a moth-shadowed bulb that passed for a guttering candle:

Hello Arch,
How are you? Work's going well. – I'm over here taking some photographs – .
But it's good to remember a nice face every now and again. Here's to peaceful
Moseley and Little Bill coming through the window! And here's to poetry!
Lots of love,
Vee
xxx

Blimey. She'd written: nice face, poetry, love. Signed off with three kisses.

Three kisses!

What could that mean? *And why was I shaking?* I rolled a cigarette, tried to get a grip. Thought again about the loving and leaving that had taken place so many moons before Vee. About the way that Vee made me feel. About the short step from too much feeling to too much hurt. My mechanisms coughed apologetically into action. Maybe the number of kisses meant nothing. Maybe I was just reading too much into what she had written. The language of a postcard is so non-intimate that you have to hang onto the thinnest of lines and only let go when they are stretched - beyond all reason - to mean what you want them to mean. Any dummy could see there was nothing in these words but the writing of them.

Couldn't they? *Really?* Yeah, unlikely, that. This was my best effort yet I was kidding myself if I thought it was doing any good. Since Vee'd gone away I'd tried, I mean I had tried but I hadn't been able to rationalise my feelings nor blur her traces nor pass over the accompanying feeling of dread. She was still with me, a year on, in misheards on buses and fat rain on dry pavements, in the light that came from houses after dark. Clearly, I had misjudged the control I had over my feelings; clearly my defence mechanisms were failing.

Clutching blindly now, anxious to shift the focus of my response to her postcard, I considered the practicalities of the situation. So that was where she'd gone to. Split. *Split.* I'd seen the name somewhere recently. Wasn't that in the former Yugoslavia? There was a war going on in the former Yugoslavia. It was one of those things that had started after the wall had come down, people trying to sort themselves out. It probably involved ex-Communists. I didn't know much about it, I knew that much. I also suspected that this was more than most people knew. I asked

Tom about the situation, then Stripe and Sorrell. They confirmed my suspicions. Which left Plan A...

'Mike geez. What you watching?'

'Magenta Devine.'

'What's she doing?'

'Wearing shades.'

'No shit. Any good?'

'Nah, rubbish.'

'Listen Mike. Do you know where Split is? It's in the former Yugoslavia, isn't it? Do you know what's going on over there? I mean, there's a war on, right?'

'Yeah Arch, there's a war on. I saw it on Channel 4 News last night. I tell you the news is brilliant at the moment, it's great! It's the Serbians mainly, they're mad bastards, total turbo nutters! They want a piece of Yugoslavia for themselves. There's this geezer. I tell you he sounds a bit like a mini-Hitler!'

'Serbian?'

'Yeah.'

'Are we involved? I mean are we caught up in it in any way? Are we doing anything over there?'

'Not really. I think it's pretty much a family affair. Why do you ask?'

'I've got a friend who's out there.'

'Oh yeah? What's she doing?'

'Some sort of photography I think. She doesn't seem too worried about it. So it can't be that bad...'

'No, well, it's difficult to tell isn't it? I mean it's like in the Gulf War. There's cameras out there filming everything and I reckon you can tell how bad it is by how many TV people get offed.'

'Yeah?'

'Yeah. 'cause they're not cheap, those cameras. And think of all that training! At the moment, I think the cameramen count is none. So you're not even talking Gulf War yet, if you take the Gulf War as, say, three and a half.'

'A half?'

'I think there was someone stepped on a mine, lost a leg. Or two. I forget how many.'

'Yeah, suppose so. Thanks Mike.'

Oh well. Whatever I felt about Vee, I could do nothing about it, just now, absolutely nothing. I'd deal with the situation if and when she got back. Until then, I'd keep getting by as best and as convincingly as I could. The rest could look after itself.

7. Castlemorton.

'Morning Sorrell,' said Tom one day in May 1992. 'Morning Stripe. How're you doing?'
'Good, mate,' said Stripe. 'Just off to a party. Do you fancy coming?'
Tom looked at me. I shrugged.
'What, now?' said Tom. 'Where is it? Anywhere we know?'
'In the Malverns,' said Sorrell. 'We'll go in my van. You coming Arch, yeah?'
And I said: 'OK. Give us half an hour.'

~

It was midday. I began to get ready. I sloped off downstairs to stock up on alcohol. The day didn't seem special. The sun was going through the motions, it was breezy and on the breeze was more of the same. But then the sun didn't know any better and the breeze could only guess. In the off-licence, I saw Cheesy and Smurf. Cheesy was trainee Brew Crew, a lunch-out soap dodger. He was buying a four-pack. Smurf was a young traveller. They were coming up on something. It looked as though the head tunes sounded good. Their faces were ticcing in time.
'You alright, geez,' I nodded, 'geez.'
'Just off to a party,' they said.
'Oh ar?'
It was the first time I'd heard them as 'they'.

Outside, at the bus stop into town, I saw Jude and Beck. Jude wore leggings, a home-made T-shirt. Nice girl, bit dim. Just graduated in Psychology. Beck was good value. Floaty dress and para boots, showing lots of shoulder. Jude looked distracted, Beck hot and wired. I didn't know they knew each other.

''ow do. What you up to?' I said.

'Going into town to catch a bus,' said Beck. 'There's a rave on. You coming? It's about time you did, y'know. Lost your cherry.'

'I don't know. Maybe I will.'

'Well then maybe we'll see you there,' said Beck.

A car drove past. Someone shouted 'Arch!' someone else 'Beck!' The car was full. I clocked Big Tommy in the front. Maybe Ruth hanging out of the back window. They were going to the party.

It was three minutes past midday.

~

'You know what?' I said to Tom, back at the flat. 'There's strange things afoot at the Circle K.'

'What?' said Tom.

'Don't worry,' I said. 'It's from a film.'

'Stanley Kubrick?'

'Bill and Ted.'

'Tosser,' said Tom.

'Tosser?' I said.

'Moron then,' said Tom. 'I'm just trying to keep you on your toes. You ready Sorrell? Shall we go?'

~

And then Stripe is driving Sorrell's wagon, a big red Merc and Tom is in the back because he likes to see where we've come from and I'm sitting up front with Sorrell because I like to see where we're going. Stripe takes us through driftings of cherry blossom and past abandoned Moseley churches. We pick up some people I've never met and they sit in the back of the van, Finnula and Kate and Andy and Si. Everyone is smoking weed. It all smells like skunk. We leave Moseley. We are going through the edges of the city. The sun is brighter now, bright May bright. We pass flat suburbs, retail park car parks. The sun bounces off turtle-waxed roofs and square windows advertising discount kitchen tiles. I find myself thinking about the lives of these people, these other people. These people outside Moseley. They are Citizens, probably, checking their Charter to make sure they get the most out of life. This is their politics now that politics has finished. Retail parks and the Citizens Charter.

Stripe has put on a new tape from The Levellers. *'There's only one way of life and that's your own.'* It is simple, exhilarating. He drives quickly. He is brooding. I am talking to Sorrell.
'So what's this party then?'
'It's the Avon Free Festival, yeah. It was supposed to be somewhere else but the cops kept moving it on. They found a new site a couple of days ago.'
'So what's it in aid of?'
'What do you mean?'
'Who's 'they'? Who's put it on?'
'Nobody's put it on it, silly. It's a festival, yeah? A free festival.'
'I don't understand.'
'A free festival yeah? Do you remember I said there's lots of them, every year?'
'Yeah, I remember. But they can't be completely free. Someone's got to pay for them.'
'Who has? It's just travellers, people coming together, yeah? Why does everything have to be about money?'
'I still don't think I understand.'
'You'll see. Here. Do you want to skin up?'

I skin up. We smoke. We are out of the city. We drive along A-roads. There are new-builds in Barrett-named Crofts, big cars in car parks of Mock Tudor pubs. I haven't been out in the sticks for a while. Not since I was camping as a kid. I am thought-ploughed, stoned. The country is passing by slowly in the distance. The country seems smaller than I remembered it, somehow diminished. There are bright yellow fields of rape, the odd bored horse, some sane and docile cows. There are traffic cones alongside dusty verges. There are traffic cones everywhere, spoiling the scene. *Something should be done!* I think. If only someone would do something! *About the cones!* It is the suburban sticks. It is rural Britain in microcosm, other people's Britain in microcosm, microcosmic Britain, a diminished Britain. A little Britain, a listed Britain. Idling in a layby, uninspired. Complacent. Untouchable.

In the van it feels good. Stripe has sped up. It feels good drinking beer in the van. We are going faster. Everyone has begun to sense that we are going somewhere special. The Merc is noisy. More cans are cracked open. Everyone is up. I am intrigued and excited. Where are we going? What sort of a party is this? Sorrell is over-excited. She squeals at animals in fields, a horse, a donkey, a goat. Tom is more sanguine than usual. He is getting slowly wired, waiting for new connections in his brain. Waiting for the higher experience to come to him. Stripe seems on edge. He is taking us somewhere special. Kate or maybe Andy or Si passes him a tape from the back. He puts on Primal Scream sampling our take on Old Mose, sampling Peter Fonda from Wild Angels - 'We want to be free, to do what we want to do, we wanna get loaded and we wanna have a good time' - and then *Slip Inside This House*. It is euphoric and foreboding. We drive along narrow lanes past neat houses. People stand on their doorsteps and stare. We are aliens. The cabin of the Merc is a long way above the road. We swing round dusty corners. We look down. We wave. The place is bigger for us being here. There are hills, green hills, hedgerows, sheep, the van imagined blurred red and daring against the landscape. The place is bigger for us being here. We're here for a party. We're here to shake up this town.

And then we hear the beat.

The beat begins just as we round a bend in the road, attach ourselves to the end of a line of vehicles. We are in a convoy of battered vans, tape players on wheels and nippy little numbers full of Sun readers and clerks. People come past us on bikes. Motorbikes, pushbikes, scooters. The beat hits us like a thrill. It is repetitive, relentless. It is elemental. It comes out of the ground, from the earth and the hedgerows and the sides of the hills. It is human, primal.

The beat is everywhere, from everywhere and I feel it in my core.

'Is this acid house music?' I say.
'House? No way. House is that commercial shit they play at those money grabbing raves. Dance music for straights. This is techno. This is free party music. Makes you want to dance, yeah?' says Sorrell,
and it does, it does. She whoops
'Yeah! Yeah?'
and then Stripe makes a noise, Stripe lets out a roar, animal, that is deep and then screeching
- aiiiiiiiii-eeeeeeeeee-eeeeeeeee -
and then there is another turn and the van goes quiet. We slow to a crawling gape. We have climbed a long incline that has led to a common or at least what used to be a common. Now the earth moves. It is a mass of thousands of people. There must be tens of thousands of people. There are hundreds of tents,

thousands of vehicles. It is an extraordinary sight. There are flags flying. There are bodies, body parts everywhere. The scene is carnival, exhibition, open-air theatre. It is bacchanal, ritual, festival, spectacle. It is happening, congress, event. We are driving slowly through a mass of people. We are all grinning. Stripe is grinning. We pass marquees. We pass benders. There are teepees. Giant speaker stacks. Old ambulances and ex-Army trucks.

'Fuck me,' I say, 'It's just like Glastonbury. Only...'

'Glastonbury? *Glastonbury?* Fuck Glastonbury,' says Sorrell. 'Glastonbury's all about money, yeah? This is about love and respect. And party people.'

'So who are these people? Are they travellers?'

'They're party people.'

'And what are all these townies doing here? These scallies? Shouldn't they be down the pub or beating up some studes?'

'They're not called scallies. Are they Stripe? They're cheesies, yeah?'

'Cheesies?'

'Cheesy quavers – ravers. Most of them are OK, yeah? They're just here to have a good time like the rest of us.'

'If you say so. So who's organised this then?'

'Nobody's organised it. It's all organic. It's all just people doing their own thing. If you want to make music you bring a sound system, if you want to bring a sound system you find a generator, if you want to bring a marquee, bring a marquee yeah? And lighting too, Arch. You wait 'til night-time, 'til you see the lights, yeah. The lights and the décor in the marquees. There'll be lasers and all sorts.'

The beat is everywhere, sound systems playing techno. We are moving slowly. There are black flags flying. Anarchist flags. There are flags patterned with crop circles.

'The Spiral Tribe!' says Sorrell and I can only nod and she says 'they're techno-pagans, shaman. They live on the road. They're at all the parties, DJ-ing, dancing,' and I can only gawp at the sight, tho' I'm not too sure which sight in particular to gawp at.

We pass cars decorated as giant fish. There are fire jugglers, stiltwalkers. We pass sculptures. There are sculptures made out of carbits. There are sculpted giants with exhaust-pipe limbs and heads made from old TVs. Firebreathers. The scene is post-apocalyptic, medieval. Everything shakes in the heat. It is extraordinary. I have never seen anything like it.

'So who's made the sculptures?'
'Just people.'
'Just for here?'
'Just for the festival, yeah.'
'And who's done all the electrics?'
'People.'
'And they're not paid anything?'
'No, Arch, they're not paid anything.'

I see people from Moseley, people who aren't from Moseley. People from the tills of Kings Heath supermarkets, the cornershops of Balsall Heath. I see more marquees. People are playing didgeridoos, bongos. Banging on the side of the van in welcome. Offering spliffs. There are food stalls plying beans and noodles. People dancing. Whole crowds dancing. In the mid-distance over a haze of smoke and heatfug and steam and halfway up a quarry-scratched hillside there are people riding motorbikes up into the high May air and then arcing out of sight. This happens in slow-motion. We crawl on. Five minutes later and another angle and we see them across a shimmer of people, landing in a pool of water. Bikes first, flipping slowly through the air, then a welter of distant whoops and limbs.

'Look!' says Sorrell. 'There's Wango Riley's!' and I stare. A woman is hefting an amp on stage. The stage is black and brilliantly coloured.

'Wango's is a travelling stage yeah? They come to all of the festivals, put bands on. It's a converted lorry, a lorry with its side down.'

We pass two coppers in the thick of the crowd. Their helmets are off and they are playing frisbee. Someone is offering them a tray of hash cakes.

'What about the old bill? Why don't they do anything?'

And then Stripe speaks deliberately and with techno and the beat all around him and it sounds like new poetry and it sounds like a mantra from a man in a trance:

'What can they do Arch? This is public land, common land, our land. This is *our* land, *common* land, *public* land. It belongs to us all, to all of us, travellers, pagans, party people, yeah? travellers and pagans and FREE! PARTY! PEE - *PULLLLLLLL!*'

~

'Right,' said Stripe, 'I'm going to park up here. You got any drugs Arch?'

'Tom?' said Sorrell, speaking to the back of the van.

'Sorrell?' said Tom.

'Only hash,' I said.

'Have one of these then,' said Stripe.

'What is it?'

'It's a pill. A Tangerine Dream. Now watch and fucking learn.'

~

It is night. Spangly black. I am sitting on a slope with some people. I am smoking something. The beat is everywhere. Someone says:

'Dancing is a sacramental ritual that connects us to who we are. Techno is the channel we pass through as we perform that ritual.'

Someone else says

'Yeah, right on, man,'

and everyone laughs and everyone acknowledges the truth in the comment and in the laughter too.

~~~

Two days into the party, swimming with MDMA. Limbs tingling, eyes off to one side. Stripe somewhere over there. It is nearly dark. The lights have come out again. Dusk is expectant over the tents on the common. The beat is getting bigger. A rumour starts in the crowd. We move towards the nearest stage. There are two people, someone says, who've been caught stealing from people at the party. Who are they? They are scum, says Stripe. Robbers. Thieves. Muggers. What are they doing to them? The crowd is unsure. Thrilling. They're taking them out onto the stage, someone says, going to give them acid in front of everyone, take them up into the hills and leave them there. A cheer goes up. I find myself cheering. Stripe is ecstatic. There is a look in his eye that has nothing to do with MDMA. You see? he says, you see? We dance.

~~~

For two days we wander around the common and dance.

~~~

And then in the van on the way back to Brum two days later, post-ecstasyed, vital toxins trickling down the cracks in my crazy-paving brain, I thought about the party, the people and the dancing in tents with space lights and lasers and the black sky at night with explosions in the sky and how it had been a great party, the best of all parties, but also of what else it had been, how those crazy days - yes, those *crazy* days - had gone beyond parties and were more, were a coming together that you might have seen if you'd put the graft in, a coming together of dissipation and energy, of getting fucked and exploration, of me and Tom and Stripe and Sorrell, of walking through the fire and the world and its possibilities, of things that I didn't know needed to come together, disparate elements brought together by a party, by techno and the beat and of how the experience had opened my eyes and affected me deeply, more deeply than any of Tom's numpty-fuck quests for grails or chats with disinterested gods, more deeply than Stripe's anger or Sorrell's hippyshit nonsense, more deeply even than the teasing ambivalence of Mike's pissy-pants peeping-tom piss-taking or my bottomless commitment to getting by and letting the rest take care of itself.

My complacency had been shaken, I had been stirred. I'd danced, struck dumb and cheering, to extraordinary music. I'd met artists and 'sparkies' and 'cheesies' and travellers and musicians and DJs in an underground of heightened emotion that Stripe's earlier violent outbursts had only hinted at. An underground of other people, people with sound systems, electricity generators, fluorescent backdrops that glowed in ultra-violet light - people who could build stages and sculpt with fire and erect marquees and cater for hundreds - people with practical can-do will-do cheek who didn't need to be told what they could or couldn't do but were getting on with it and creating their own community and making their own sense out of the world. There'd been tens of thousands of them, boys and girls come together on a common in the Malvern Hills for fuck's sake. And of all of the tens of thousands of revelations that had flipped slowly through people's over-heated heads those sun-baked, e-cooked and star-bright days and nights in the hills, this was mine...

Our Moseley was finished. Plum tuckered out. Gone and then gone some more. Up against the energy of Castlemorton, our Moseley was suddenly tired and soft, a rag-tag duffle-bag of throw-back strung-out half-soaked punked-up bohemiedom with nothing to offer but more of the same old stories and fucking and self-indulgent chat, more of nothing but the safety of pointless party on pointless party; nothing but the fag-end of an attitude, a once-wild ride dusted down and ridden like a mothballed helter-skelter on light nights where nothing much was asked for and not much given in return...

And then,

in the back of the van,

Vee came to me,

in the way that she did,

in the way that people do when you are dust-happy,

happydazed,

in your cups or high on life

and with her came that extraordinary stillness,

that harmony, that goodness

and no matter that I was dust-happy,

happydazed,

I wished that she was here

with me.

8. A.C.

After Castlemorton everything changed. It didn't take long either, I mean not by the standards of your average inside-outing of the entire cultural-political landscape. Stripe said that it was as if we'd started a fire and the whole country was going up in flames.

We had the press to thank, of course, for the speed at which we took hold. By the time we arrived back in Brum there was a blur of images from the party on the national TV news and we had already been smeared all over the pages of the papers. It seemed as though the whole of diminished little Britain had been shaken from its complacency, stirred as one listed mass to repel the ten thousand, twenty thousand, one hundred thousand aliens and reject their alien notions about the freedom to party and be happy and have a good time. Castlemorton had been the biggest free party the country had ever seen. And the reaction of the press was furious and unprecedented.

Mike, naturally, absorbed it all, his fingers pecking at the remote control and tearing paper as he turned the pages of news and opinion. The piles of print marking his sofa-space grew and - not wishing to waste an opportunity to leave us even less sure of his motivation or intentions - he used them to essay an apparent rapprochement with his former bête noire.

'Look mate,' he said to Stripe, 'no hard ones, yeah?'
(I noticed the 'yeah' and that he'd gone with Stripe's 'mate' not our 'geez'. Whatever he was after, if anything, the boy was a piece of work.)
'I was only taking the piss. I mean, y'know, credit where it's due. I didn't realise you were so... I mean I didn't realise you would

make quite so much noise... I mean, fucking hell, you're legends you are, you're major-league – what's the word? – *celebrities*. Well, obviously you're *not* celebrities but you know what I mean! You're everywhere! Look at this. Farmer Giles with his shotgun. It's just like Viz! *Get orf moy larnd!* Fantastic! Front page news, you're front-page news! Like those American pit bull terriers! Tearing up the place! Fair play to you, mate. Have you seen this...?'

He shook a small newspaper. It was the Daily Mail.

'I've bought this because you're there on the cover. And inside an' all. Listen to this. It's an interview with this, er, geezer, 'Willie X'. What a name! Willie X! Do you know him?'
'...' said Stripe.
'He's supposed to be a cheese of sorts. Public Enemy Number fucking One by all accounts! Listen to this:
'It is the ability of the travellers to use the laws to their advantage by targeting common land that has made them so successful and so infuriating to rural communities in recent years. A glance round Willie X's flat shows a textbook on the constitution and copies of The Independent newspaper.' The Indie-fuckin-pendent, mind!'
'Jesus,' I said. 'A textbook on the constitution? And The Independent? Call the cops.'
'That's not what they want. They're talking about bringing the army in,' said Mike, 'to stop you lot trashing the place again...'
'...!' said Stripe,
'...except of course it says here, in the small print, that you haven't trashed anywhere. Listen to this: 'the environmental health officers from Malvern Hills Council moved onto the site to begin clearing refuse and praised the travellers - *praised the*

travellers - for their help, saying it had halved the cost of the operation.' So you've not done bad, PR-wise, if anyone's prepared to read the small print. Here we are again: 'Assistant Chief Constable' - *Assistant* Chief Constable. Oh well, better than nothing I s'pose - 'Assistant Chief Constable Colin Davis said: We have been supplying them with plastic bags and they have been using their own trucks to bring rubbish to the skips.' Fair play to you mate, I mean fair play!'

It was difficult to gauge the success of Mike's approach to Stripe but it was undeniable that the ink-blood in the water was enlivening us all. It was entertaining reading papers we'd never read before, being kept amused by the hysterical inaccuracies they were peddling as badly written fact. Not to mention the perversity of it all. None of this was supposed to be happening. Not now, not after Thatcher and Numpty Frank. Not now, with John Major and that Spitting Image slug and the fat one, whoever the fuck they were. Arguments like these were supposed to be over. This violence of opinion was supposed to be over. We were supposed to be just getting by. It wasn't supposed to be like this.

And yet it was. Over the next week or so, Mike continued his ambiguous woo-ery - 'it's like reefer madness all over again. Or the Rolling Stones! Look at this! No-one's got a clue what they're on about. 'I've told you once m'lud, it's a popular beat combo. *A Popular. Beat. Combo!*'' - and Sorrell chuckled at the news that 'hippies' at the party had been accused of trying to down a police helicopter with a flare gun. Stripe bought a Daily Mail, cut out a headline - 'These foul pests must be controlled' - and Blu-tacked it, anarchist-style onto the fridge that stood on our shaky kitchen floor, whilst I contributed a handlebar moustachioed admonishment of 'hordes of marauding locusts' which I'd found in a copy of the Telegraph that someone had left on the bus. We all began watching the news more often too, just to see what they would cook up next. Mike said that 'the news was getting better' and I had to agree. I had never really watched the news like that before, as part of it. We liked to think we didn't care about attracting such disapproval, but we did. This was the flip side of the bad press. It was novel to be noticed and it was good.

Stripe certainly thought so. As the response to the party grew ever more fantastic, he jacked his ranting up to a new level, his brooding times were fewer and the earnestness with which he used to negotiate the buzz of his do-something *do-anything* days was replaced with a god-freak zeal.

'I tell you what, what you saw at that party,' he said, one particularly voluble afternoon, 'it's just the tip of the iceberg. The thing that gets me is that we're told that we have to work in some shitty little office or that we shouldn't be signing on and that we're no good for anything, but look at what we can do when we come together as a community. And they're shitting it that we can come together without their sayso or their laws, come together and do our own thing. They just can't get their heads around the fact that there's no-one holding the purse strings, that it isn't about making a fast buck but part of creating an alternative to all that shit. It's not about their way of doing things any more. Their *politics*. Their politics are finished. Knackered. They've had their chance and blown it. It's not about them anymore, it's about us, it's about us and what we can do. It's about a whole new approach, a whole new way of doing things. Going back to the old ways. We're not trying to get into the future. We're trying to get back to where we were before we fucked it all up. There's so many of us out there, I tell you, just up for changing the world. Helping ourselves, creating communities. It's fucking DIY, mate, it's DIY culture. We can make a difference doing it our way. And things are going to change.'

At this exhortation Mike nodded knowingly and Sorrell yeahed. I bunted my bifter and tried to stay calm. This was just what I needed to hear. At Castlemorton I had glimpsed a thrilling alternative to what I knew about the way things were and could be. An alternative way of thinking and doing. An alternative common sense approach to making sense out of the world. I wasn't too sure what it was or where it might lead but I needed to find out. And, since the party, the efforts of the press had served only to exaggerate the urgency of my need. What would it come to mean, this coming together at Castlemorton Common? Could it be that Stripe had some of the answers I was looking for?

It certainly seemed as though he might. Before the party I hadn't understood his anger. In isolation, with our old Moseley simpering boho posey all around, it had seemed unnecessary and I had considered the boy a simple-minded sort. Now I saw that I had just been too passive, too lazy to engage with him. And that his anger was just a part of what I had seen at the party, a part of what was going on.

Only Tom seemed unimpressed. His relationship with Stripe appeared to have taken a bit of a knock with the experience of the party and its aftermath.

'Yeah, but what does it *mean?*' he asked when Sorrell and Stripe had left the room, 'any of this?'

'It's difficult to say geez, it really is. But you've got to admit they're having a pretty concerted pop. Maybe they're scared of

something. Something from the party. Us, maybe. I don't know geez, I really don't know. But I'm keeping an open mind.'
'But Arch,' said Tom, pained, 'there's nothing there. It's all just kid's stuff. Can't you see that?'

I looked at him sadly and shook my head. It was a shame for the boy, examining his midriff on our old sofa bed, his frame curled into a question mark as he considered his next acid-laced offering. I'd maybe have agreed with him once but this was no time for the bathetic nuances of his flights of existential fancy.

I mean don't get me wrong, Stripe had only *started* to make sense. A community in which partying was the reason to be seemed a bit low on usefulness even to an inveterate head like me. And his DIY version of what would replace the old politics seemed a bit bodge, codge and plastic wood. One morning he got on one about something he called the 'Information Superhighway' and how it was going to break down the system, give power to the people and change the world.
'We're going to start making history all over again,' he said, quoting someone whose name he'd forgotten. I was instantly reminded of Mike's chat of earlier in the year that Stripe had dismissed with such vehemence and couldn't help but consider his transformation from atheist to evangelist an unconvincing one; at least, that was, until I remembered my own not-so-distant admiration for the wink and the distancing shrug.

That was the point and Tom had missed it. Criticising Stripe for making an effort was too easy. If some elements of his chat were a bit shonky, at least he was offering an explanation for what I had experienced on the common. Someone had to. Because after Castlemorton everything had changed. And the only real question was how.

I began spending more time with Stripe. He was less into the drink than Tom and when he was up and riffing he spoke energetically about hunt-sabbing and the unnecessary evil of vivisection. His chat was harder work for both of us right enough, but he got me into more parties than Tom had ever managed.

The focus that summer was on parties in disused properties: an old print shop in Balsall Heath, a derelict bank in Highgate, closer to town, an old photographic studio in Mose. There was talk of an illegal solstice bash in newly squatted buildings down the smoke. 'Why leave buildings empty,' said Stripe, reasonably enough, 'when they could be put to good use?'

If - by default - our parties were now acts of political dissent, they were more professional too. They had to be. There were no more home-made compilation tapes, stretching minutes into hours with clever segues from Dylan to The Stone Roses. Now we listened to techno. We expected more. The parties had DJs, lights and light-reactive décor. If the decks were in a back garden, there'd be a marquee. Whole groups of people worked together to get a night on, technicians and artists, DJs and crew.

Not forgetting the old bill of course. The backlash from the state was about more than just words. The outnumbered, accommodating bumpkin coppers of Castlemorton had long since returned to cycling through morning mists and boxing fictional scrumpers' ears. In their place were city filth, chomping on steroids and grinding feelings of inadequacy between their teeth. And your party was nothing without at least one explicitly threatening visit from these comedy jokers.

Sometimes it was over noise levels. Or it was a raid for drugs, with dogs. The biggest 'mare was when they'd turn up and threaten to have the PA away, or confiscate the DJ's rig. As a consequence, people throwing parties started charging on the door. It wasn't much - two or three quid tops - but it helped provide some insurance. For some of the old skool, this was a controversial shout. Once, Stripe tried to get all four of us in for the price of two and Tom complained about the very idea of an entrance charge.

'I've never paid to get into a party and I'm not about to start now,' he said.

'Come on mate,' said Stripe. 'He's a good DJ. You'll like it. It's only a couple of quid.'

'That's not the point,' said Tom with an unusual smile. 'What about 'free party people'?'

'Ah come on now, mate, now you're taking the piss. Do you know who you sound like? Mike, that's who, sat at home in front of his telly, Micky no-mates, just taking the piss. It's different when it's someone's yard, you know it is. What about the lights, what about the décor, the backdrops, what about the PA?'

'Whatever you say,' said Tom.

He turned away with an un-Tom-like shrug and headed back up the hill towards Moseley.

He was going nowhere. There was a new rhythm to our dissipation and Tom and our old Moseley were out of time. We had no need for its bohemian comforts now. We even had our own drugs. We'd always taken speed as drinking powder but now 'e' was everywhere too, an eternal gurn. Before Castlemorton it hadn't been a Moseley thing. We'd always seen it as the drug of the fashion victims who lived up Kings Heath. First it had been too expensive, then too disposable, too much the choice of straights and part-timer townies playing at weekends. 'Acid for people with no imagination,' as Tom had once snorted. Only now were we becoming privy to the nuances of its language, less written or oral than unspoken on buses and in front of the funny boards down the dole, alive in the eye-moves and smirks that told of the new coming together and of the dry-ice and smoke-filled rooms of our new gathering places.

That summer our old gathering places didn't put up much of a fight. Within a couple of months of the end of Castlemorton, the council demolished the Victorian bogs in the centre of the Village to make way for faux Victorian street lights. Matching bollards were installed. The Cocks shut for refurbishment. It was a listed building but the rumour was that they were gutting it, turning it into a theme pub. The pavement outside, where we used to mill at weekends, was being narrowed for a wider slip-road and more fast cars. Trucks and lorries now drove over land where we'd partied. Pedestrians were given short shrift, the life of the place, given short shrift. This was a corporate theming, a violent act against Moseleyism. It should have been anathema to old Moseley; it may even have been to our Moseley, before we were distracted. Yet in The Prince, punters picked at the subject of the closure of The Cocks like pigeons at breadcrumbs. It was a desultory kind of reflex-nostalgia, a going-through-the-motions sense of loss.

The other side of Moseley started to lose its appeal too. The Traf shut. The dealers slid down the hill to Balsall Heath, the punters started using The Bull's Head. The Bull's Head was in Moseley, it was a Moseley pub. But nobody spoke of it. It was full of sex-offenders offering duty-free fags, old women dribbling. At the bar slumped ACAB-tatted bad men with no time for the la-di-da ponces of the erstwhile Wild-Westest boozer in town. In the Bull's Head, come autumn, you could rent the full

Remembrance Day kit from Irish Dave, knock-off Sally Army cap, shaker and home-made poppies, five for a pound. The Bull's Head wasn't romantic. The Bull's Head was shit. Tom was the only person I knew who'd ever been happy drinking in there, amongst 'real people' 'who'd given it a go', 'it' being - as far as I could make out - the breaking of a glass into the face of anyone who turned up their noses at packets of knock-off Lambert and Nasty that tasted of fag smoke.

None of this was us, not after Castlemorton. Our horizons were broader now. That summer there were parties in the sticks as well as Balsall Heath, gatherings in old quarries and fields in Wales and the lawless border country. We'd set off from Brum in trucks and jeeps and landies and bangers, winding around narrow roads, down dirt tracks and lanes and paths of shale. Some of these parties were little more than a single sound system, a marquee and a coil of gaffer-taped cable. Some attracted 200 plus people. Then there were the bigger tear-ups, the mini-Castlemortons and Sorrell's original free festivals, the Forest and Harvest Fayres, where hippies would dance to techno and ravers wig-out to bongos. There were Teknivals too, in Pembrokeshire or The Golden Valley. Here techno-pagans showed us alternative technology. There were lights powered by the wind or people pedalling a bike connected to a generator, audio-visual installations using old television sets to create illusions of infinity.

We'd arrive to the welcome of the beat and the unspoken greetings of acquaintances as friends, Beck and Finula, Jude and Big Tommy and Ruth, wired with bonhomie and pills. Then we'd dance. Just dance. We'd dance until the dew dried and the police choppers appeared, low over the hills and squat like fat flies.

Yeah, the coppers got out into the sticks as well. Especially into the sticks. It was a real piss-take. I mean as a smoker, I'd never had much time for them but this was different, a barely credible campaign of rabid harassment and banana republic style violence and intimidation.

Since Castlemorton it was almost as if it had become illegal to have a good time. Spiral Tribe threw a party outside the Canary Wharf complex down the Smoke and were busted for their pains, for daring to dance. A convoy was broken up in Powys. Sorrell smoked free draw for a week on the back of a typical encounter with the old bill at a garage just outside Hereford. 'They opened the back of the van and they had these dogs, yeah, these sniffer dogs and they were going mad. I had to swallow my stash.'

At the Torpedo Town Festival in Hampshire, Stripe told us, he'd even been arrested as they'd tried to frame travellers for a fire that had gutted a nearby council building.

'If they keep pushing us,' he went on, 'something's going to crack' and it was difficult to argue with the boy, even as I was still unsure what would happen when it did.

Truth be, despite being told what I wanted to hear, I was beginning to feel unsure about many of Stripe's pronouncements. '*He has the conviction of the dim*', Tom had said and his Simple Simon certainty was beginning to make me uneasy. Notwithstanding an occasional rhetorical flourish to the contrary, Stripe's DIY politics seemed to consist of a series of objections to the status quo, a comforting fester of antis. He'd spoken of 'creating communities' right enough, but 'how' was a question that still floated. As much as I'd tried to cut him some critical slack, as much as I'd wanted to believe - and I wanted to believe, really I did - his vision was a bit blurred. Where was the substance that would bring it into focus?

And then in August, even as his chat was losing in authority what it was gaining in volume, the discourse moved on to a whole new level, a level to justify the noise each side was making.

In August Stripe introduced me to some friends of Sorrell's who'd been at Castlemorton. They were called Simon and Clara and Laura and Ig and Billy and that spring they'd set up some sort of protest camp near Winchester at a place called Twyford Down.

'They're planning on building an extension to the M3,' explained Ig. 'It's going to go right through this area of special scientific interest, an ancient burial ground and an area of outstanding natural beauty. No respect, I tell you, these people have got no respect. Except now there's a whole bunch of us down there going to make it very difficult for them. We're living in benders, we've got a camp going on. There's a tribe called the Dongas too. That's what these ley lines that run across the Down are called. The Dongas.'

The road protesters had come to Brum to fire people up and chill. We saw a lot of them late that summer. They all wore utility belts and talked about chaining themselves to diggers or trees. Ig did most of the talking. He was the lithe side of scrawny and calmly enthused. He spoke quietly. He could do. He'd lived on the road for a year before joining what he called the defenders of Twyford and his words came coated in the resultant charisma dust. He was a thinking man's Stripe who was everything, in action and chat, that Stripe imagined himself to be.

Ig talked about non-violent direct action. Building tunnels under land state-tagged for pneumatic drills. Living on platforms in the branches of trees. Anything to stop the road builders, now the likes of Friends of the Earth had bottled it. He talked about the connection between the protest and the parties. About The Levellers and The Diggers and their struggles over ownership of common land. He didn't know much detail about this stuff right enough, but then I wasn't after a history lesson, just something to hang my hat on. He was hot too on freedom of association, the right of people to gather together. A group called Reclaim the Streets and their opposition to the cult of the car and the system that promoted it. The Spiral Tribe and how 'free parties are shamanic rites which reconnect urban kids to the earth' and how an understanding of these rites would help to avert the 'ecological crisis' that was just around the corner.

One time he showed me a copy of a newsletter called Squall, out of London. It was full of news of squats and squat parties and international squatting. It pointed out that there were hundreds of homeless people sleeping rough in the capital and thousands of empty houses. It was on cheap paper and skewiffly put together but fuck it, this wasn't a sheet of Tony's borrowed doggerel nor even 'angelheaded hipsters', this was ours and urgent and now.

'It's all part of the same thing,' Ig said one evening as we sat mulling, 'squatting, travelling, us down there protesting about the road. It's all to do with living our lives the way we want to, not the way that corporations, big businesses, the government, vested interests want us to. It's about freedom. It's about having control over our lives. And they don't like any of it because they can't control it, except through violence and repression. Do you remember the Battle of the Beanfield?'

'What's that?' I said.

'The coppers smashed up a traveller convoy on its way to Stonehenge for the summer solstice. Bunch of hippies they were, not causing any harm to anyone. But the state didn't like them because the state couldn't control them and so the state arranged for an ambush. It was really bad. There were trailers destroyed, vans destroyed, women and children beaten up, I mean really battered. A reporter for ITN - *ITN mind* - said he'd never seen anything like it. Even the Lord whose land it was on said it was bang out of order. Grotesque, he called it. It was all filmed as well - and the coppers nicked the footage! There were pregnant women getting battered over the head, kids in trailers getting covered in glass, people hospitalised. Seriously! Pregnant women getting hit with truncheons. And you can't see it now for love nor money.'

'Shit. When was that?'

''85'. That was where a lot of this started you know, that was when a lot of people started to get involved, thought they could make a difference.'

'You see, that's the thing. I don't think that I, I mean I don't think that many people these days think they can make a difference, not really.'

'Yeah, that's a popular misconception,' said Ig. 'We make a difference every day in everything that we do. Believe me.'

'I suppose you're right,' I said.

'From the moment we're born we're up to our arses in action and can only sometimes guide it by taking thought.'

'Who said that?'

'I forget now. But he makes a good point.'

'...and what about the poll tax?'

This was Stripe now. Scowling, confrontational.

'Shit, yeah, I suppose so,' I said. 'Were you there?'
'At the riot? Yeah. We showed the bastards then I can tell you. That's what I call direct action, you know? That's what it's all about, changing the balance. Put a few people in hospital, make sure there's less of them polluting your air, that's the only way you'll make yourself heard.'
'So what do you reckon about this Castlemorton thing?'
'What do you mean?' said Ig.
'What do you reckon they'll do about it?'
'I don't know, yet, but there'll be laws. They'll think of something. But whatever they do, we'll be ready.'

There'll be laws. He was right an' all, they were on the case. A Tory Minister called the Twyford defenders a bunch of 'alcoholic anarchists.' 'These so-called travellers,' said one know-nothing bufton-tufton on Channel 4 News, 'are a direct assault on the structure of social life in the country.'

And then they did think of something and soon Mike was reading from the Guardian that some government minister had promised new laws 'in reaction to the increasing level of public dismay and alarm about the behaviour of some of these groups.'
Give Castlemorton its due. Just six weeks earlier I wouldn't have cared what some government minister was saying. And now? Some of these groups? That was us.

That was us? So, this then was how things had changed after Castlemorton, this was what the coming together had come to mean. There were no longer travellers and squatters and road protesters and free party people, we were all travellers and squatters and road protesters and free party people. People who would say 'no' to lives in flat suburbs or Barrett-named crofts, to calls to cones hotlines and to Citizen's Charters, to the desecration of the countryside and state-approved fun. People who demanded an alternative.

This was the final ironical flourish of those crazy alchemical days on the common. We hadn't asked for any of this. We hadn't asked to be vilified. We hadn't asked to be goaded into believing stuff. All we had done was gather to dance and get loaded and have a good time. But with every attack on our freedom to do as we chose came another point in our context, until our new identity had coalesced like a Magic-eye tree. And now, now we were no longer defined by drunken quotations or tied by lines of poetry to old history and energy spent. We were no longer once or twice-removed. Now we had a vision we hadn't been looking for, a purpose we didn't know we needed.

This was why they were scared.

Because we had made a new and different sense of the world. Because they'd spoken of the end of politics and they'd hoped that it was and yet they were wrong. It was just the end of *their* politics and as they spluttered their last, it was our time; as their politics finished, ours - organic, multi-faceted, unpredictable - were just beginning.

And we were what was coming next.

Autumn came and with it came squally rain like polemic aligned in diagonal lines and then autumn sunlight like tangerine dreams. Two years on from everything stopping Stripe was playing us bootlegged Radical Dance Faction and it felt as though we'd only just started.

'Society needs to condemn a little more,' said John Major, 'and understand a little less. New age travellers? Not in this age! Not in any age!'

And we were defiant and angry and united in our righteous anger.

9. Sarajevo zoo.

The next postcard arrived at the flat, in an envelope with a note. The postmark was blurred and there was no date so I couldn't tell where it had been sent from or when.

The envelope was addressed to 'Arch, The Flat above Victoria Wine, Moseley' and I was unsure how she had got even that much of my address. It must have arrived here via some kind of celestial sorting office for all of the correspondence that gets sent out, improperly addressed, into the ether.

Whatever, it was good to hear from Vee again. No, it was better than good. However much I'd initially hoped that I would remain young, free and on the charge, I'd changed. My once failing mechanisms had failed. I'd realised that on my way back from the party, when she had come to me in the van in the stillness and I had again experienced the harmony that I knew from the night we had met.

I was ready again, I saw that now. Vee wasn't Geraldine, never had been. Vee was no-one I'd ever known. She was different, beautifully, implacably different and no matter how much I'd tried to deny this I'd known it from the moment we'd met.

And I liked different, different was good. It mattered, there was no use pretending it didn't. That was what would make the two of us special. And I was ready, again, for love.

I read her postcard first. It was an old postcard, probably from before the end of the Cold War. It showed a dam on the river Drina. The dam was made of concrete and it looked bright in a Communist sun. There was dense forest at either end of the construction. There was a small map that showed the course of the river along the border between Bosnia and Serbia. Had she chosen it specially? And if so, why? Knowing her as closely and intimately and deeply as I did...it could mean absolutely anything.

I read the postcard first.

Dear Arch,
I hope this finds you well. I'm ok out here but looking forward to coming back soon. Work is good but play is not so good. After what happened in May I hope things will change. Please stay safe and keep getting into trouble!
Lots of love,
Vee
xxx

Still three kisses. No change there then. So that was all right. And what did she mean about May? The Bank Holiday? Could she have known about Castlemorton? Could she? There was no reason why not. She'd certainly have access to newspapers. Blimey. The message was spreading across the whole continent!

Then I read her note.

'ps.
I forgot to say, strange as it may seem, I miss you Arch. Sometimes I'd like nothing more than to be there with you in Moseley, just chilling out, listening to music. I often wonder what sort of music you are listening to now. The music over here is intense. Some of it I'll be able to hear forever but I'm not sure that is a good thing. I really hope I can be back in Moseley soon and we can have a smoke together. And who knows. Maybe even listen to some more Walk on the Wild Side...'

With these words I shook my head and fuck me if something wet and tear-like didn't land on my duvet. Bless Vee. God bless her. *Walk on the Wild Side?* I couldn't remember the last time I'd listened to the Velvets. I smiled. It was ironical - there was that word again - that she was missing chilling out with me at exactly the time that I'd begun to throw myself into the world and its possibilities. She had been right about that, I could see that now. There was more to life than just getting fucked. The world didn't revolve around me. And while it was obvious from her note that she wasn't expecting me to have risen to her challenge, she'd be impressed, I was sure, with my new engagement with the political.

As well as our resistance to a draconian state, I'd recently begun to pay some attention to what was going on in the former Yugoslavia. It seemed only right, with Vee over there and all. I'd seen on the news that the Serbians were still fighting the Croatians and now the Bosnians were fighting the Serbians. I'd also read about the Serbs being big bearded party heads and the Croats making a virtue of their sobriety. And then of course there were the animals starving in the zoo in Sarajevo. They'd caused an enormous fuss! All over the press that had been, that bear in particular.

Even so, I knew that this was just the beginning. I needed to know more.

'Mike, geez. What you watching?'
'London's Burning.'
'What's it about?'
'London's Burning? This enormous flood.'
'Sounds great. Any good?'
'Nah. Rubbish.'

'Have you seen anything about Bosnia recently?'

'This about your girly friend again?'

'No. I mean maybe. I mean – anyway, what's going on?'

'Well there's Sarajevo. You know, where they had the Winter Olympics? You remember. What were they called? Those skaters. He was gay, she was a cartoon pig...'

'Torville and Dean?'

'Boreville and Preen, that's them. Sarajevo's shot to shit. But don't ask me why. It's Serbians and Croatians and Bosnians and anyone who can lay their hands on a gun as far as I can see. Muslims as well, for what that's worth. They're all turbo nutters, Arch, don't you worry about that. You'll never work out what's going on though, so you might as well not bother. Come to think of it, you never used to bother. Why start now?'

'I don't know. I'm past that not bothering stage. There's more to life than taking the piss you know.'

'Such as?'

'Oh, I don't know. Connecting with people. Y'know, Mike, other people. You might want to try it some time, it's good for you. I mean answer me this. Are you happy?'

'Delirious geez. Why do you ask?'

'Just wondering.'

'So it is about your girly friend! And in case you hadn't noticed, I like taking the piss.'

'Yeah, but Mike it's not just about you and what you like doing. It's about us, you know? All of us.'

'What does that mean?'

'I'm just trying to make a bit of an effort, that's all.'

10. Me and Tom and Sorrell and Stripe and Ig.

That summer, Tom and I drifted apart. On the few occasions we crossed paths we managed to miss each other. Even on cloudy days he seemed touched by the sun.

I wasn't sad about the demise of our friendship, not any more. There was no need. His contrariness in life and naiveté in love frustrated me still but he seemed good enough on it. And the mischeviousness that had accompanied my abandonment of him to Sorrell's rapacious mercies had given way to a genuine hope that he would continue to seem good on it.

I still had my reservations. Some concerned Tom and the way of his world. Most were centred on Sorrell and the uncomfortable feeling I'd tried to subvert ever since she'd spoken of us being similar in character. Her words had struck a dissonant chord. Whatever makes you happy Arch, she'd said. Deep down Arch, we're both the same, she'd said, there's no point trying to deny it. You're not kidding anyone, she'd said, be yourself, yeah? Just be yourself. What's wrong with that?

It depends, my little free-love head, it depends. Plenty, if you look too closely.

Her attitude to the Twyford lot as they traipsed up to Brum for hospitality and moral support was of particular interest. She'd hey-yeah-wow them one-by-one and happily sit through a communal catch-up and burn but as soon as the talk turned to the practicalities of the protest, she'd hitch up her floweries and skip off to the next wow-no-yeah? This was not the behaviour of one whose intentions were strictly honourable.

Something for nothing, that was what Sorrell wanted. Not in terms of material things of course. She didn't care about material things. When the Sue Ryder shop in Kings Heath was out of hippy chic, she shopped at the British Heart Foundation. But peace of mind, happiness, entertainment, a sense of herself. Peace and Love. She wanted these and more for nothing, as her right. That was hippies for you I suppose. They don't see the graft you have to put in.

She was wrong about me and her as well. We may have been the same at one time. Party-fucks ago-go. But despite her chat, there had never been anything else to her, not really, whereas selfish wasn't me anymore and I'd moved on from something for nothing. Belatedly goaded by her attempts to emotionally implicate me in her machinations, I even ended my games with Tom and tried to speak to him about their relationship.

He'd come into the living room one morning as I sat and smoked and gawped at the telly. I was ready for him that morning. Fuck, was I ready for him. I'd been up all night on a combo of bad chat and zippy medicinals and now Mike Morris was on TVAM. The programme was poor. Mike Morris lacked charisma. It was as though someone had just locked joe-punter in the studio and pointed the camera at him in the name of entertainment. TV couldn't get any worse. I didn't ask where Tom'd been. He seemed as though he was out of it. His hands were stiff and cut and bloody. He said he'd picked a flower for Sorrell and that her favourite colour was purple. He was carrying a thistle. Its woody stem was frayed in strips to the marrow. It had ripped his hands, cut through his skin and into his flesh as he'd tried to twist and pull it from the ground. I'd pictured him pulling at the stem, in the dark, demented spines and twisted plant fibres tearing his flesh and him oblivious to what it was doing to him, his back bent and his eyes wide, his hands bruised and thick and bloody and I'd winced.

And then I'd asked him why he was doing what he was doing and if he was happy. He spoke distractedly.

'I never used to believe in happiness. I always thought that happiness was atrophy. But it's not y'know geez, it's some trip.'

I'd said:

'I know we haven't been that close lately and it might be none of my business, but I've been a bit worried about you. I mean I didn't know it was your thing. You know. The whole...*woman thing.*'

And he'd said:

'What? And it's your thing? Here's your thing. Newspapers. All the news that's fit to print. Just kid's stuff, Arch. Children's games'

I'd said:

'Yeah but women, geez, I mean people, I thought that all that people stuff was beneath you, I mean I thought it wasn't your thing. You do know she's still seeing Stripe?'

And he'd said:

'I know. It's not about them, it's about us. Sorrell's not like other women, she's a free spirit. We're like boy and girl, lying in the grass or playing cosmic games in the weed-grown park.'

'Fuck me. Tom?'

'She says I've got the strongest pheromones she's ever experienced.'

'Yeah but Tom, mate, I mean come on. When did you last have a bath?'

And then he'd said:

'Everyone's just playing children's games, everyone who isn't on this trip. You're playing children's games Arch, do you know that?'

and I'd said:
'You just take care Tom. Tom?'

There was no talking to the boy. I'd always thought there was nothing his head couldn't take, nothing that would flip him out. Now I wasn't so sure. He was off on one, not so much misreading the situation as living in a world where there was no situation to be read.

Half a moon later I was at a 'party' with Stripe in a lock-up in Digbeth. Stripe had begun to brood again recently. At first I didn't know if this was because he saw Tom's moping as a challenge or he'd had his beak put out by the ease with which his position as the authority on the new politics had been taken by Ig. Either way, this particular Sunday we were waiting for an anti-climax after a hard weekend and the party was doing the business. It was an ambient affair, playing intelligent dance music. People had just started chill-out nights like this for those of us who'd been up all Saturday, giving it large. Or thems that couldn't take their techno in the first place. The music was feebly-weebly bleeps and nurdles, the soundtrack to dolphin porn. There were light sculptures, a café selling cake. Home-made visuals, with air pumped through a film of oil and water between two sheets of plastic, projected as bubbles floating up the walls. People on gentle acid and pills, looking at the texture of each other's clothes. Discounts, no, straight-up, *discounts* for people bringing cushions. I was just about to go home for a snooze.

Stripe had come back from Brighton. Sorrell was supposed to have gone with him but had chosen instead to spend the weekend in Brum. With Tom.

'Were you with Sorrell's lot,' I said, 'the Earth First!-ers?'

'Nah mate. Not really my scene.'

'How so?'

'Put it like this. There's people who think they can change things by non-violence. People like Ig. They'll tell you about Ghandi and Martin Luther King. They're 'fluffy'. And then there's people who know that you're only going to change things with direct action. If you know what I mean. Malcolm X style. We're 'spiky.''

'And Sorrell's flirty? I mean fluffy? Sorrell's *fluffy*?'

'Right on both counts.'

'But you work your way through it?'

'I don't know about that. Let's just say, I've got no problem with it. Y'see the thing is Arch mate, I might come across as very easy-going, y'know, very easy to get on with,'

'...'

'but you don't want to piss me off, not really. I love the woman, you see. It might not be very obvious but I love the woman Arch. I love the woman so much it burns. And if you play with fire you're going to get burned. Do you know what I mean?'

'Absolutely geez,' I said. 'Good party isn't it?'

Later that night I thought about Stripe, his kickboxing, his entirely justified sexual jealousy. About his burning love, that burned. A chimp with a broken typewriter could have done better than that, but then Stripe was never really about poetry. I thought about quietly-spoken Ig, the potential for conflict between the two of them. Then I thought about Tom. By now he'd have learnt any lessons he was going to learn about his cavalier attitude towards our friendship. Yeah, maybe it was time to start looking out for Tom again...

And then I thought about me. Truth be, there were more important things on my mind than getting noised-up by old skool silly business fuck-games. Such as what else these interesting times were going to lob in my general.

11. February 1993.

A bad time, that's what, a terrible time. This winter is cold. This winter outstays its welcome even as it announces its arrival. December stamps into the city carrying placards and our placard-composition freezes. Rebellion is more of a stretch when you're suffering from seasonal affective disorder, fighting back tricky when you've got a chill.

On a day we will come to call Yellow Wednesday, hired thugs from Group Four Security come for the Dongas on Twyford Down. After three days of violence and thirty plus Group Four resignations over the level of violence used, the Dongas are evicted, their benders cut to pieces. There is nothing about the attack in the press. Most people have come off the road for the winter. We are struggling to keep our fight in the public lens, losing our momentum. Our confidence is fragile. Are we losing the argument?

More worryingly, given the newness of my conversion to a life of supposed activism, my confidence is fragile. Over the winter I have scuffed around basement techno nights, keeping warm with ecstasy and speed. I have danced, defiantly, I have partied, radically, I have taken underground drugs in clubs under the ground. But to what end? I am unsure again, uneasy once more. Techno is the soundtrack to what is going on but is that it? Is this enough? Ig had shown me there was more to DIY than partying, but what part did partying play in DIY? Was there something in what Tom had said about 'kid's stuff'? Tom, his head flipped by a flibbertigibbet and confusedly hypocritical with it, was nobody's idea of a reliable witness...and yet...this dancing...these *shamanic rituals*...could it be that he was right after all? What to think? What to believe?

~

Winter is long this year. It is February now. I miss Vee and keep an eye on the news. But it is half-hearted. I know enough about the world to know it is all I need to know. Some nutters hole up in a place in Texas, a bomb goes off in New York. Some Arabs have tried to blow up the Twin Towers. I don't know about the nutters in Texas but you've got to love those Arabs.

~

Sorrell and Stripe come back from Twyford the following weekend. The camp is getting back together after the eviction. Sorrell says it has been odd, Stripe hasn't been with her, he's been sniffing around the security guards and the portacabins of the Department of Transport contractors. It is now that I see Stripe start to set fire to things. I am coming out of the private park on Monday morning and I see him in the alleyway that runs behind our flat and round the back of the shops. He has set fire to something in one of the big metal rubbish bins. The flames are thin, curling around the top of the bin. They sneer. For some reason I think about the fire at the Torpedo Town Festival. Stripe sees me and says 'Go about your business, Arch' and I see a look on his face that I haven't seen since Castlemorton. When we caught that mugger. This is not a reassuring development.

I think about mentioning something to Sorrell, but what? That afternoon Sorrell says to Tom 'shall we go out?' and Tom doesn't answer and Sorrell says to me 'what's got into him?' Tom has got it bad. He is lovestruck, dumb like an animal. He has barely left his room all weekend.
'I don't know,' I say to Sorrell, 'don't you?'

I go for a walk with Tom to see if I can snap him out of it. We go to the offie, pick up a couple of pick-me-ups. We sit with the jakies on the benches where the grass used to be. There are lots of them today because the flophouse on Wake Green Road has just shut as part of Care in the Community. They are all over the Village, pissed-up or mentally ill. It is cold. There is a lacerating wind and I say to Tom, 'come on geez, let's go back inside', but Tom just sits.

I miss Vee and Mike isn't helping. 'You need to kick back, take more drugs,' he says, 'that's all that's expected of you. Be more Generation X about it all. How you used to be. Leave changing the world to others! They'll be better at it than you anyway, trust me. I saw in a magazine the other day this cartoon that's going to change the world. It's huge! It's a spoof American sitcom. It has a go at absolutely everything. And I mean everything! There are no sacred cows, dude! It looks brilliant!' I humour him. 'Uh-huh?' I say, 'how's that then?' 'Haven't you heard how taking the piss is a powerful thing?' says Mike. 'It's called satire.' 'What's the name of the cartoon?' I say. 'I'll be sure to look out for it.' 'Beavis and Butthead,' says Mike.

'Beavis', I say.
'And Butthead.'

Despite his proclamations to the contrary, none of Mike's information gathering is making Mike any more powerful. He lives off takeaways from The Pacific Fish Bar next door to the Cocks. He has made an arrangement with them whereby he collects his tea - a bag of chips and a Fleur de Lys pie of the day - every night at 7. Mondays, Tuesdays and Thursdays is steak and kidney, Wednesday and Saturday chicken and mushroom and Friday and Sunday minced beef. It is difficult to know which is more indiscriminate, Mike's absorption of information or his absorption of mechanically recovered meat.

He has begun spending money on clothes, ordered from a catalogue and delivered to our door. He is working hard on a look. It is grunge from the pages of Kay's. His pallor is convincing. He is pallid. It is the bad meat. But I tell him he has maybe missed the point, that grunge is about how you live your life rather than how you look. He says, yeah, like everyone who dresses like Kurt Cobain is on smack? He says there are millions of people all over the world whose only experience of life is what they see in magazines or on the TV. Are they wrong to try and belong in this way?

Mike hardly ever leaves the house. The last time he left the house was to go and see Reservoir Dogs. For the third time. He is not a bad man. He does not build roads or bust parties. He consumes inconspicuously. He is not yet the enemy, at least not as far as I am concerned, partly because I am not too sure who the enemy is any more and partly because even if I was as sure as I was a couple of months ago, he would always be less of an enemy than a gap between two enemies. But it is now February. It has been a shit winter. I am antsy. I used to go with the flow, like Mike. But there must be more to going with the flow than this.

One day he is sat there with a book. 'Fuck me geez,' I say, 'that a book?'
'Aye,' says Mike. 'Right enough.'
'I'm sorry?'
'You doss radge.'
'*What?*'
'You always said I should read a book, and so I am. You doss radge.'

'What the fuck is a doss radge? And what's the matter with your voice?'

'Ah tells ye, wait a bit, ken this is, er, hang on a minute, *barry*. Everyone's talking about it! You should read it! It's almost as good as Reservoir Dogs!'

'Hmm. 'The best book ever written by man or woman,' eh, '...deserves to sell more copies than the Bible.' What's it about?'

'These chancers. You'll love it.'

I read it. It is a good book. We would like it to belong to us but it doesn't, not quite. We take all sorts in Moseley, we dance alongside all sorts, some people even take a puff of poppy, but we don't do skag - except with voices of superior concern - and we don't do AIDS. This isn't our life. Reading it I feel inexplicably guilty. We are once-removed again.

And so is Vee. I miss Vee. I am unconvinced by the situation. I begin to question. It's not as if she isn't here anymore. The space she should be filling is full of the space that she has left. But who is to say someone else couldn't fill that space?

There is a situation developing with Sorrell. It is complex. I love Vee and I miss her and I am starting to feel resentment. She is wasting time that we could be wasting together. Are there other men? I sleep with other women.

In March, I meet Sarah, a one-time part-time girlfriend. We are in The Bull's Head. I haven't slept with Sarah for three years. I don't fancy her. She doesn't fancy me. We fancy each other like we fancy a fuck. It is last orders. My cock is full of whisky, my mind is tired of ennui and my heart is already set on the hair of the dog. We come back to mine. Sorrell is there with a geezer.

(Tom is speeding with Pigeon Park punks, Stripe kickboxing in Cov.) It is a desultory business all round.

The next morning I meet Sorrell in the kitchen. Sarah has long since gone. The tape player is banging out Debaser by the Pixies. It is not Sorrell's music, I think. But then anything is Sorrell's music if Sorrell is listening to it. Sorrell is empty and endlessly if not deeply self-aware. I don't know if this is healthy but it is an interesting combination. I think that lots of people are hippies without even knowing it.

Sorrell spreads two slices of toast with some soya margarine. Offers one to me. I don't know what this is supposed to mean. If I was offering her a slice of toast it would mean that I was flirting with her. I miss Vee and Sorrell is very fanciable. I start to think about sleeping with Sorrell. I might even slip on some Pentangle to help get those hippy juices flowing, not that she will really listen to what I put on, not that music will really get her juices flowing, she is, deep down, more prosaic than that.

And Sorrell is very fanciable?

Jesus.

It is time Vee was back.

This winter is bad.

12. Allaying suspicions.

I met Ig in The Clifton on Brighton Road, in Balsall Heath. It was a straight-up boozer with no pretensions or qualms. The door of the bar was open onto the street and polystyrene chip trays blew in. A barman was looking at horse racing on a TV at the end of the bar, shading his selections with a biro in the Sun.

It was early and we were the only people in the pub. We were drinking Guinness, our feet on the rail that ran along the bottom of the bar. I was hunched over my pint, playing with beer mats. I wanted to talk to Ig about my renewed sense of unease about our DIY enterprise. I had been wondering how I was going to phrase it and what he was going to say.

I said: 'So what gives then, with Twyford. I mean do you need more people down there...? Or...I mean...have you got enough...?'
Ig looked puzzled.
'We always need more people down there. The more the merrier, yeah? Why. You thinking of coming down?'
'Not as such. I mean I'd like to, it's just, you know, finding the time... The thing is, I've been thinking lately...about what you're doing, about what *I'm* doing. I mean I'm with you all the way, don't get me wrong. I just feel as though I'm not really putting the effort in, you know? There're things I could be doing and I feel as though I'm not, I feel as though I'm just winging it.'

Ig shook and dipped his head. He looked disappointed. I took a nervous and deep swig of my pint, afraid that I had let him down and anxious to smooth over the feeling. Ig gripped the bar with both hands then he turned away from me and began to speak, exasperatedly at first and then with more measure and in his words I heard a riffing, pre-complications Tom, an evangelical Stripe, a dewy-eyed Sorrell...

'I think you're missing something Arch. You shouldn't be asking me these questions because none of this is about what I think. We're all winging it, that's the point. I mean yeah, sure, we could do with more people at Twyford, of course we could, a hundred more, a thousand more. But it's not just about stopping the roads. It's a state of mind. It's about people like you Arch, thinking for yourself and doing what you can. Taking responsibility for the way you want to live your life. That's what's going to make a difference. Don't worry about what other people are doing. All you can do is take responsibility for yourself.

And you've got to be positive Arch, you've got to believe you can. You've got to demand the impossible. I know that this can seem a bit much at times. You want to try spending a winter on site, that'll put it all into perspective for you. But look at it like this. You go dancing, yeah? Well every time you go to a free party or spend a dollar in a club that isn't charging ten bar on the door and turning the taps off so punters have to buy bottled water, you're making a difference.'

He stopped, ordered two more pints. We had the barman's full attention now, his eyes flitting shiftily from me to Ig and back as he waited for the Guinness to settle. He was unsure what he was hearing but then what was he going to do about it? We were the only people in the pub, after all.

Ig continued, brazen, talking about the legalisation of cannabis. He said that the act of buying and smoking was another difference I was making, if only I knew it. He said that as long as the black market continued to grow, the pressure to pass laws to take advantage of the demand and control the supply of the drug would become irresistible. This was DIY as improvisation, thinking on your feet. We would use the system's own rules to make it easier to create an alternative.

As he spoke I glanced back at the barman. He had returned his attention to his paper, interest spent, more fool he. Like he'd never smoked weed, like it didn't concern him. We'd see.

'And what about everything else?' said Ig, 'smack, 'e', the lot. Why not? It makes perfect sense Arch, on every level. You take out the snide pills, the stuff that's cut with weedkiller, let people know what they're dealing with. Straight away that's cut down on the chances of people od-ing or going bad ways. Then you issue licences to whoever wants to sell it. Tax it all too. Like fags. Fags are legal. What's the difference? Fags kill you. Fags kill a fuck of a lot more than 'e'.
Can you imagine it? No? I didn't think so. It's impossible. But that doesn't mean we can't make it happen. We can make it happen whether it's at Twyford or the Forest Fayre or the Cooltan squat, we can create an alternative. So you keep 'winging it' Arch. You keep on keeping on, doing what you can, taking responsibility for your life. These are your choices you're making. Because it's not up to anyone else is it? No-one else has the right to tell you what you can and can't do. No-one else has the right to tell you how you should live your life. This is about the freedom to do what we want. You just keep the faith. Do you hear me geezer? You just keep the faith.'

He punched me lightly on the arm. It was a gesture, rather than a statement. I hadn't needed to ask if I belonged. As he always did, Ig had done a bang-up job of allaying my suspicions about the usefulness of what I was doing, of the part I had to play. And as the barman pressed home his pen and his indifference, my face relaxed into a shit-eating grin. We finished our pints and left. The sky was the bluest and although it was brisk for April and litter pirouetted in the wind, it felt good walking home and I wondered how I had ever been unsure.

13. A day and a half.

One year on from the day I went to Castlemorton, one year and another of the anniversaries that had begun to stud our lives like matchsticks in shit, I was at a party in an old curry house on the road that separated Moseley from Balsall Heath. Now that we were weary of the jejeune, the kiddish, the merely pissed and stoned, now that we had wearied of the reminiscences of the whiskers in the Prince of Wales, Balsall Heath was where we gathered. It was real down there amongst the sari shops, the halal butchers and neon-shouty kebab houses, the happy-clappy black churches and mosques. It was real and grown-up and full of the world and its possibilities. Geezers called it the ghetto, shopkeepers chewed qat, crack was the offer of the week. In spring, the sun didn't catch blossom but broken glass. The existential fires we saw or pretended to see from a distance burned all the day long, in the eyes of people who'd never cared much for the poetry of the flames. The cars had darkened windows. The partying was fierce.

Winter had been a blip. A hiatus. A downer. Then spring came. I'd spoken with Ig and my questions had stopped and I was convinced again. We *were* what was going on and I had to do my bit. Because we had work to do. Whatever they were thinking of was getting closer. We could smell the legislation. Not that they needed it. That week in May alone there had been numerous state-sponsored attacks. There had been a mass arrest at Twyford Down. Fifty seven protesters were nicked by two hundred riot police for occupying part of the construction site. Punters leaving a festival in the Forest of Dean had been surrounded and filmed by the law. 'Operation Snapshot' they called it. We'd heard of a road scheme in south London. They were planning on destroying old Oxleas Wood for the sake of another bridge across the Thames. Meanwhile, a party at Cosmo's lock-up on Brighton Road had been busted, his PA taken down the station.

That spring there was a renewed purpose to our dancing. We were defiant again. Our partying was political once more. Party-goers and party throwers were, once again, at the centre of a country-wide campaign of civil disobedience and direct action. We were eager for the next move. The next provocation, the next killer tune. *There'll be laws?* OK, OK. Bring it on. *Because whatever they do, we'll be ready.*

The party in the curry house was in a long narrow room where the buffet tables used to be. There were blackouts hanging from the walls. The music was uncompromising, techno for the purist. It had thumped its way from Detroit to Frankfurt to Brum and now it was ours, techno for the activist and the answers in the beat.

I was at the party with Sorrell. We were together by accident. Tom was at home, skint and sulking like a martyred mooncalf. Stripe was 'out', likely fomenting armed revolt, not that I was taking the piss, at least not seriously. Sorrell was annoying me. She'd decided that I wanted to sleep with her and that tonight was the night. She was possibly right and probably mistaken. I wasn't too sure in which order.

I was uneasy about Sorrell but I had a good feeling about the party. It had the makings. We had arrived early and there were only twenty-odd people there but you wouldn't know it from the DJ who was giving it large. Already there were homies sloping, dreads flicking sweat. Already the bass was in my veins.

'This music,' shouted Sorrell as we skinned up on the edge of the dancefloor, 'there's not much to it, yeah, not much crescendo.'

'It's techno. What do you expect?'

'I don't like it. Have you got any of that black on you?'

'Not on me.'

'Shall we just go back for a smoke, yeah?'

'No. I've just had half a wrap of speed. I'm not in any special rush to leave. Why don't you go and talk to Tracey?' I said. 'I think she's out the back.'

Out the back was a chill-out room and Sorrell took the hint. I was glad. I was there 'till the morning, to dance and get sweaty. I wanted shot of her. And besides, I hadn't decided about sex with her, not yet and I didn't want to have to make the decision tonight. There was Tom to think of. The logistics of it all. Stripe. Maybe Vee.

Maybe Vee? Nah, not this early in the night. I could never let Vee get that close to me, not this early in the night...

And then I saw her.

Jesus.

Standing further along the wall, a strobe light freeze-framing her movements as she rolled a cigarette.

Vee.
Jesus.
Vee.

I walked towards her and she looked at me and mouthed

'Hell - oo',

the action sucking the energy from the room and vacuuming in a whomp the months she'd been away. There was a pause whomped months long and then I sobered up, right there, I sobered up and felt my heart flush, my heart empty and fill.

'Hello Vee,' I said,
and then 'HELLO VEE',
and she said
'LET'S GO,'
and I nodded.

We left the party. It was a light night but ordinarily so. There were no portents in the elements. We didn't need any. My ears were buzzing. I could still hear the beat from the curry house. All we needed was now. I stopped to sit on the bonnet of a black-windowed Beemer and sparked up the spliff. It tasted too sweet. I put the spliff out. I didn't want it. Everything was bright and shiny at the edges. It was just us and the night was brilliant at the edges. Vee didn't say anything. She looked beautiful but different too. We started walking.

'How long have you been back?' I asked.
'About two days,' said Vee.
'Why have you come back? Was it because of my face?'
'It's certainly an unusual face.'
'An unforgettable face.'
'An unfashionable face.'
'I should say.'
'So what brings you down here anyway?' said Vee. 'I mean I knew I'd find you here, I asked a few people about people. But I was surprised. I didn't think it was your thing, paying to get into parties. In Balsall Heath.'

'Ah, but Vee, time's change. My world's got bigger since you went away. I don't really go out in Mose anymore. Not much.'

'But you still live there?'

'For the moment. Above the old butchers. Where are you staying?'

'With San. But she hasn't got much space.'

'You can stop at mine if you like.'

'Yeah, thanks, I'd like that.'

We walked in silence for a block or two. I shook my head and grinned at her. She looked at me grinning. I saw now that each time I had pictured her these last months I had got the odd detail wrong, until her face and body was a composite of what she was and what she would never be. Even now, looking at her face as we walked through a light May night, there were features that I still couldn't be sure about. The precise colour of her eyes or the exact shade of her hair. None of this mattered. She was beautiful.

'It's funny,' I told her, 'for the last two and a half years I've had this dialogue with you in my head. I've kept up a running commentary on what's going on just to see what you'd think about things, how you'd react to stuff that gets my goat or makes me laugh. And now you're here. And I can't think of anything that I want to say. No, that's not quite right. That I need to say. But... The funny thing is, I still want to talk. Do you mind that? If I just talk?'

This time I thought *she* grinned.

'Carry on,' she said, 'please do. It's nice. Makes me feel comfortable. As though I haven't been away,' and then of course I couldn't think of anything else to say.

We walked on through Balsall Heath, past initialled veg shop shutters, blue and green curry houses, Zaff's all-night kebab house in dim and lurid yellow. I ate there sometimes these days on the way back from parties in Highgate. Masala fish in naan or spicy chicken wings and fries. There were puffas sat at the long counter. Under neon, like Hopper. I wondered if we should stop at Zaffs, if I should show Vee a bit of my bigger world. I thought about telling her about what I'd been up to, about showing a bit of interest in what she'd been up to. A spot of compare and contrast. I didn't know much about the woman but historically this had been us, the hither and thither, the to and fro.

'Do you remember?' I said, 'when you went away? What you said about politics and how you couldn't stop it, you couldn't stop trying to make sense of the world? It almost felt as though you were setting me a challenge. *Go away my son and try to make some sense out of the world*. Well we've all got politics now Vee, all of us. So what about you? What have you been up to? Making sense of the former Yugoslavia? Were you in Croatia? Or was it Bosnia?'
'Both. At times. Taking photographs. I was working for an agency.'
'And was it good photography? I mean, y'know, what was it like over there?'
'What was it like?'
'Yeah. I mean did you see much of the war? Did you want to see much of the war?'
'I was photographing the war for the agency, if that's what you mean.'
'Well, yeah. OK. But you see...'
'Arch? Do you mind if we don't? Tonight? I mean just for tonight? Do you mind if we talk about something else?'
'Like what?'

'I don't know. Like normal things. Your favourite films, or, or
TV programmes. You could fill me in on all the gossip if you
like. I'm sure there's lots of gossip.'

'All the gossip?' I said. 'That doesn't sound like you.'

'Time's change, Arch. Do you still see Irish Kev?'

'Nah.'

'Annie and Mick?'

'Annie and *Vic*. Mick's seeing Liz.'

'And what about Big And?'

'Yeah, he's still here.'

'Little Bill?'

'Doing time I think.'

'Medium-sized Pete? Average Joe?'

'Pete shrank. Joe isn't average any more'

'I see,' said Vee. 'And what about you? Do you still quote
random lines of poetry?'

'Gawd bless you no. I don't do poetry anymore. Techno is the
new poetry.'

'Are you sure?' said Vee.

'Absolutely. Think about it. It's common sense. Back in the day,
when we were living in caves, it wasn't words that got us dancing,
that got us connecting to the starry dynamo of the whatever. It
was rhythm. The beat. Well that's what techno is. The beat. It's
poetry with all the unnecessary stripped away, reduced to its most
basic form.'

'Oh dear,' said Vee. 'It's a convincing argument alright, but
believe it or not I was looking forward to a bit of your quoting.'

We walked up the hill towards Moseley Village, past people
picking up momentum as they headed into the ghetto for the
night. Vee asked me who I lived with and I said to her 'Jesus,
you'd have a field day with them' and she asked why. I told her
about Stripe and his furrowed brow and his anger and how 'in

another life he'd probably be a copper' and I surprised myself by saying this. I told her about Mike and how he believed in most things and fuck-all. I told her that Tom was Tom and that he was above politics and that politics couldn't provide Tom with any of the answers he was looking for.

'I don't think he's a well boy. He's mad with the lust. You know, that kind of nutter-lust that some people get?'
'Nicely put.'
'Thank you.'
'Who with?'
'Who with what?'
'Who is he in nutter-lust with?'

and then for some reason I didn't know what to say. Just as I was wondering why, someone shouted 'Arch!' from a way behind us and I recognised the voice and sobered up from sober. I turned to see Sorrell running up the hill.

'Ah,'
I said quickly,
'speak of the devil,'
too quickly.

'You didn't tell me you were going,' said Sorrell.
'Sorrell, this is Vee. A friend of mine.'
'Ahhh, I see. Hello Vee. Any girlfriend of Arch's is a friend of mine,' said Sorrell, smiling an unwholesome smile. 'Anyhow, yeah? I suppose I'd better be getting back to the party. The music's a bit more chilled now and D's just turned up with some black.'

Sorrell skipped back down the hill with a 'see you both' over her shoulder and Vee said

'What did she mean by that stuff about 'any girlfriend of Arch's'?'

I looked at her, half-hoped she was being serious, couldn't tell. I ignored her question but I don't think she noticed.

We walked. I wanted the walk to go on. We took a turn off the main drag. It wasn't the most direct route home. Vee clocked it. There were trees. I asked her

'Why did you come back, Vee? Down here I mean. Tonight. To me?'

and she said

'For the same reason that anyone ever goes back anywhere. Because you're there.'

'Well now that's charming.'

'In a good way though, Arch, you're there in a good way. You've got a nice face, you're smart and you're funny. I mean that's very attractive in a man...'

'...?'

'...'

'Is that it?'

'What more do you want?'

'What about smart and funny and, say, serious and meaningful?'

'Be careful what you wish for, Arch. Serious and meaningful isn't all it's cracked up to be, believe me. Stick to what you know, going with the flow. Leave a bit of space between you and the serious and meaningful. There always was one, after all. And maybe I was wrong to suggest that you tried to fill it. Maybe it suits you.'

'Yeah, thanks for that Vee. Once maybe. But like I say, I've changed,' I said.

And then I said:
'I love you, you know,'
this unplanned and blurted, like a child in a playground trying words. And then I don't know if it was the billy or the smoke or something else but I felt sick and the feeling of nausea took me back to a time before techno, to poetry and something frightening in the fabric of the dark of the trees against the sky when there was light all around, when we were surrounded by light that was bright and brilliant at the edges. There were portents now alright, portents in the dark poetry of the shado...

'Don't be daft,' said Vee. 'You don't love me. You just love the idea of filling that space of yours with something you can call profound. Something that seems to be profound but is actually just a bit more diverting than the usual.'

Then she said, visibly tiring of the exchange, 'Listen, Arch, I'm not being funny. But do you mind if we don't sleep together? Tonight I mean? Do you mind if we just *sleep* together?' and I was surprised, partly because she was asking and partly because I didn't mind, not in the least.

~

That morning I started out of a half-dream and saw Vee. She was sitting upright on my mattress on the floor. Her form was ghost-like. I wondered who she was, why she was there.
'It's OK Arch, it's only me. I'm here. I've just not been sleeping very well lately.'
'What? OK. Yeah. No, that's OK. What time is it?'
'It's early,' she said. 'Do you mind if we talk?'
'OK. No, that's OK.'
'Tell me about your favourite films.'

'*What?*'

'Your favourite films,' she said, 'tell me about your favourite films. I haven't seen any films in a long time.'

~

Later I was woken by Vee getting dressed. There was sun in the room. I lay on my mattress and watched her. I looked at the sunlight on her arms. Her shoulders. Her breasts, warm underneath the t-shirt she had slept in. She pulled on a pair of jeans. I heard the denim, cool over her thighs. She bent over. I looked at the contours of her body, the way her jeans clung to her curves, softly snug and round and up between her legs. She picked up a pair of socks from the floor.

'I'm just off to fetch a paper,' she said.

I didn't know she'd noticed that I was awake. I watched her as she left the room.

Some minutes later I heard her leave. I stood up, to look down at the street below. I opened the window. The air was thin. It was going to be a hot day. Vee came into view, looking around. I didn't want to let her out of my sight. She headed for the road, crossed by the bus stop.

I watched her.

She looked good.

~

That afternoon, Vee fetched a rucksack full of clothes from Sandra's. While she was away I stayed in my bedroom and thought about the previous night. She'd had a pop during the hither and thither when I'd half-joked about watching and re-watching *Bill and Ted's Excellent Adventure* and *Weekend at Bernie's* on video.

'Aren't they children's films?' she'd said.

'Maybe. No, actually. And what if they are?'

'Everyone seems to like children's films these days. No-one seems to like proper, grown-up movies.'

'Like *Betty Blue*?' I'd suggested and hadn't known whether I was being serious and she'd said 'Yeah, sure, like *Betty Blue*,' and I wasn't able to tell if she was taking the piss. I told myself it had been just like old times, such as they were and it might have been, it really might have been, I wasn't sure.

It was funny, what she'd said when I'd told her I loved her. That I liked having her around because she was diverting. She certainly kept me thinking about who she was. But what was wrong with that? She'd also said that I was looking for something that seemed to be profound. It was that 'seemed' I liked. What could be more profound than what went on in my head, whatever went on in hers and the relationship between the two?

Not that I was very sure about any of it. Some of the chat last night had been good, but for most of the evening it was almost as if she wasn't really there, as if our exchanges were on autopilot. She'd been reluctant to talk about where she'd been, what she'd been up to. And she'd been none too forthcoming about the way she felt, either. I told myself that it had been a good thing that we felt comfortable with only one of us opening up. It was only natural I suppose. There must have been some heavy shit going on in Bosnia. And Croatia. Unimaginable really. And she'd done both, the poor girl. What a head-fuck. No wonder she was a bit shellshocked about being back.

Even so, it was frustrating, what with all the news I had. I wanted to tell her about my political awakening and how I'd gone about trying to make sense of things. About how being involved in politics made me feel good about myself. And to ask her if she thought that was why people got involved in politics in the first place. She'd like that chat. It was smart and funny. I wanted to tell her how I'd never seriously considered sleeping with Sorrell, or at least if I had it was because I missed her, Vee, without realising it. How now she was back, everything had changed. I wanted to tell her that I meant what I had said. That I loved her. I wanted to tell her about how we were what was coming next and how me and her could be what was coming next too...

That afternoon we went to the Kwik Save that had opened up where the Tesco used to be. Tesco had pulled out after the jakies started to sleep in their doorway. I showed Vee the No Frills beans at 6p a tin. Moseley was struggling. It was grey and sombre. It needed re-imagining. It needed lights and dry ice and techno. It needed me and Vee.

We crawled through the hole in the fence and went for a walk in the private park. Sat on the grass and looked at the lake. Then we headed back for some food, popped into the bakery for some bread, the deli for celebratory olives. Vee seemed happier than she had last night.

Back at ours, something was occurring. The living room was full of people, Stripe, Sorrell, Mike and Ig, the rest of the Twyford lot. They were perching on chairs they'd moved in from the kitchen, sitting on the edge of the sofa and squatting on the floor. The room was very smoky. The TV was on with the volume off. Everyone seemed tense.

'What's going on?' I said and Stripe said 'the news is on in a minute. They've just brought charges against the people they picked up at Twyford. All public order offences. Nothing violent, nothing at all. I tell you, they're taking the piss.'
'This was what I was talking about Vee,' I said. 'This is what you've been missing. This is the sort of thing that's been going on.'
'What?' said Vee, as we both sat on the floor, 'what's going on?' and with that the room became a cacophony of voices:

'...we're living in a police state...
...no-one's safe...
'they're trying to stop it all, parties, festivals...
...democratic protest, civil disobedience...
...people need to know what's going on...'
until in the smoke and the fog of chatter Stripe stood up and began to speak.

'I tell you what needs to be going on,' he said and then he frowned, a glacial shift. Everyone in the room was jittery. Expectant. Behind him the 6 o'clock news had started. Mike had turned up the volume. The item was about the war in the former Yugoslavia. There were peace talks in Washington. It looked like good news. Someone with white hair and narrow eyes was talking about 'safe havens', 'a just solution.' I could just hear Stripe over the top of the TV.
'...what needs to be going on,' he said 'is direct action, people on the streets, people showing the pigs and the bastards in power that they aren't going to take it any more...'
On the TV someone was saying, more quietly,
'...complete ineffectiveness of the international community...'
'...that if they carry on taking fucking liberties with our rights, they'll have more than civil unrest to deal with, I can tell you...'

...I heard the word 'betrayal'...

'...and it won't be the fluffies they'll have to deal with, because this? *This?*' said Stripe,

'this is war.'

I squeezed Vee's hand and looked at her, wanting to gauge her reaction to Stripe's anger, to our outrage. Had she been back long enough to get a proper handle on what was going on? She had half-turned her head but I could still see it in her face and the way she was suddenly holding herself, a realisation, no, more than that, an *acceptance* of what was happening to us. But what was happening to her?

'Vee?' I said and I was surprised when she said nothing in return.

~

She woke again that night. She was sitting on the edge of the mattress, her back turned to me. I could hear her rummaging in her rucksack. She pulled out a book. It was big and flat like a photo album. She sat there and looked at it in the dark. I could have leant over to see what was in it but I didn't know if I should and I went back to sleep instead.

~

The next morning, Vee was back to her inquisitorial best.

'So why is everyone so excited?' she asked. 'I go away leaving a bunch of bohemian cynics and come back to find you all foaming at the mouth.'

She was sitting on the end of my mattress, filling my room with the unknown world. And *fuck*, she was right. I was excited.

Her dalliance with the withdrawn had unnerved me but now she was back. I answered her in a rush but glancing sideways as I went, keen to take my opportunity yet anxious to avoid any of the gaucherie of the night before last.

'It's called DIY and we're excited because it's big. I tell you, the whole place has gone up and it isn't just in this country either. All over Europe, Holland, Germany, all over Europe people are trying to create alternative communities. It all started a year ago with this free party. It was the biggest there's ever been. It was amazing, I'm not exaggerating Vee, it was a life-changing experience. It went on for about a week in the middle of nowhere and 100,000 people turned up. Nobody organised it, not as such, it just happened and there was techno and food and, and *art* and sculpture and when there was trouble we sorted it out ourselves and then we all helped clear up and went back home until the next time. And the establishment felt threatened Vee, really threatened. And they've been having a pop ever since, coming after anyone associated with the thing - restricting freedom of movement, stopping travellers travelling, clamping down on squatters, busting free parties, coming after anyone with an alternative lifestyle, anyone who thinks a bit differently about how they want to live. Ig reckons they'll bring in laws to stop the parties. And they've got to legislate to protect their road-building too. Do you know that this government has planned the biggest road-building programme since the Romans?'
'I see. So what are you doing about it? This repression?'
'We're keeping on keeping on, Vee. Exercising our rights through non-violent direct action. We're squatting and travelling and partying and making music, protesting and holding it down. Keeping it fluffy...'
'...I see. I think...'

'...yeah, I know that 'fluffy' sounds a bit facile, I thought so too, but it's not, it's important, Vee, believe me. You'd agree if you'd seen what's been happening.'

'I see... but this 'creating alternative communities'. How are you actually going about it?'

'How are we going about it? Well, it's not about hierarchies or structures for a start. It's a state of mind. It's about doing it ourselves, thinking for ourselves and getting on with living our lives the way we want to rather than the way we're told we should. It's about freedom. It's what you said, Vee - do you remember? - about not being so passive and lazy?'

'Yes, I remember. Well it's nice to see you're so, so...*engaged?* Oh I don't know, maybe I was wrong to hope you wouldn't have changed. You look good on it, anyway, Arch. This social strife...'

'Why thank you,' I said, now flourishing, 'I tell you it's good to feel part of something. And we'll win as well, all of us. We'll win. The roads won't get built. The music will keep playing. Because we can't afford to lose. This bunch, everyone talks of them as being nonentities, grey men, clueless, flapping about. Well they're not. They're shitsuckers, Vee, vindictive, dangerous bastards. I mean all this is because of a free party. *A free party!* Can you believe it?'

'I can,' she said. 'It's your 'end of politics'. Which incidentally translates as 'end of history.' Which incidentally is the most ridiculous short-sighted rubbish I think I've ever heard. But then people will buy into any old rubbish so long as it's cheap enough.'

'Yeah, good point. It's like Big Malc says. There's no communism any more, is there? And just because god – or in this case the devil – is dead, people don't stop believing, they just start believing in anything. I suppose politicians have got to justify their existence somehow.'

'Ah yes. But that could apply to you lot, couldn't it? The believing in anything bit? There you are, sitting around, getting bored with getting by...'

'No, no, no, not at all, absolutely not. I mean it, Vee, we're not playing games here. When we're out there protesting against roads, stopping empty properties going to waste, putting on parties, putting ourselves on the line, we're defending our communities, defending basic human rights. "When they came for the gypsies" and all that. Well they're coming for the travellers now, that's exactly what they're doing.'

'Interesting,' said Vee. 'Your comparison of John Major with the Nazis...'

'OK, not exactly. But it's all relative isn't it. However much you try and argue that one Vee - and I have tried, believe me - it *is* all relative.'

'Maybe,' she said. 'Maybe.'

She paused.

And then she said:

'But Malc is wrong about god. God isn't dead. I've seen him alive, in burned-out churches and mosques.'

I stopped then. I nearly answered but then I realised what she'd said. This wasn't a 'to' waiting for a 'fro'. I was disappointed and then fine. It was her experience and she'd had the opportunity to share it with me. Twice. If she didn't want to, that was up to her.

Since we had first met I had assumed that alongside Vee I had something to prove. That there was something about my engagement with the world that was lacking. I had been, I suppose, a little in awe of her ardour.

This feeling had grown during the time she was away. I saw that she had been right about the nonsense that was 'the end of politics' and right to suggest that there was more to the world than I had previously allowed for. *Walking through the fire* was about more than just getting by.

Now she was back and in explaining to her our politics, I had a new-found confidence in my own sense of the world. And with this, an alternative reality hoved slickly into view. Maybe I'd had it right as well. Maybe I'd had it right from the moment I'd first pondered the challenge she'd set me, from the day she'd fucked me and disappeared. What if she was over-complicating the issue? Maybe, just maybe, she didn't make any more sense out of the world than I did. Or for that matter than Sorrell did, or Stripe or Ig or even Tom or Mike. Maybe she had her politics - a relentless inquisition, an inquisition with no end and no beginning and I had mine - Do It Yourself and create an alternative. Maybe, in principle, there was no difference between the two, or at least none that I had to worry about...

I started. Vee had been quiet too. She tightened her shoulders, breathed out deeply, turned to look at me. I looked at her eyes. Imagined I could see into them. It was almost too much, as it always had been. Even in my excitement there was something that made me sad. I caught myself. I would make her happy.

She said 'come here a minute Arch,' and I went.

~

That afternoon I said to Vee 'You do love me really? Don't you?' and she said 'Do you know something? What's not to love?'

And when I realised what she'd said I thought about it and then I said 'Jesus, Vee, *Jesus*, you fucking beauty, you absolute *fucking beauty'* and in that moment I knew that there were no more questions anymore about Vee and the sense she may or may not have made or what she may have thought about the sense that I'd made because we were meant to be together and *she* was now the answer to everything. And the answer was yes, just yes, a great and simple yes, an inexorable, life-enhancing, unconditional *YES*, the word repeated, vital and proud then pumping, softly, like heartbeats, like a pulse, the affirmative affirmed with every dying sibilance and then pounding, like techno and the beat and in that moment Vee was the answer and the answer was yes and she was there and we were meant to be.

14. Showing Vee.

For the rest of that summer every day was a hundred Castlemortons. I was whacked-out on Vee, cloud-surfing, a pig in shit. For the first week, we stayed in my room and made love or crawled into the private park and fucked in front of ducks. We signed-on sardonically, joshed around the supermarket. We talked of recent times, as we had at the beginning. Vee asked me why I tolerated the idea of a private park, the private ownership of land, here, on my doorstep. She said it contradicted much of what I had to say about the world. In response I told her that this was why I loved her, this chat of hers, this profound and diverting ball-ache. I preferred to speak about the way that I felt, urgently and with little regard for the sensibilities of the checkout staff in Nasty Save, the punters behind the desks in the dole office. I gave Vee the edited highlights of me and Geraldine, told her how it had all gotten a bit on top, how I hadn't been grown-up enough to handle the situation, how I'd changed. And what would I do differently this time? That was easy. I'd been thinking about that. She was obviously an independent person with her own strong ideas...so I'd let her be. Space, that was what she needed. That was what anyone needed. I told her that in any case, this, now, me and her, just *was* different, a whole new man-woman experience with everything magnified, inexplicably, made bigger, infinitely.

I told Tom I was in love. It seemed important, so that he could see how it should be done. But then I wanted to show everyone how it should be done. 'Have you noticed I've started whistling?' I said to Vee. 'Whistling like a dervish. I haven't whistled since I was a kid.'

We laughed too, as only two people fucking for England could. Our senses of humour complemented each other well. As my chat turned to the relative demerits of cock burn and fanny chaff, Vee drolly demanded that we get some fresh air. She wanted to see Moseley, she said and I was happy with that. I wanted to show her how the old place had changed, to introduce her to the new parties, the new party people, the new politics. Not because I needed her approval, mind, because I didn't, at least not in that way, not now the what-ifs and maybes had become yeses. But because this - my politics and my Vee - was now my life and I wanted to share them both.

So I took her visiting. I showed her the squats that had opened up on Willows Road and Willows Crescent. I knew some people in them, Mac and Col and Ellie and Snug. In terms of amenities, the squats were pretty basic - cold running water, some electricity, no gas - but there were plans to get them connected and make them legit. There had already been parties to raise funds and in the meantime the tatters were out tatting, Mac and Ellie looking for furniture in skips, spare materials from building sites. What they couldn't knock-up from other people's junk wasn't worth having. There were lamps in Mac's room, made from nightlights in beer cans that had been twisted and slit and hung together like mobiles. The light from them spread like warmth up the walls. In her old place, Ellie had furnished a room with a four-poster bed she'd built out of old beams. If this was an alternative to the mainstream, it was hard to see why it should be.

They told us they had their beadies on other properties as well. There was an old Housing Association building lying empty in Highgate, an outbuilding of the derelict Sorrento maternity hospital in good nick. Snug had recently spent a lot of time in the squats and cafes of Amsterdam, checking it out, seeing how the scene over there had come together and grown. 'People just need to show a bit of imagination,' said Ellie, 'and we can really change the way things are done.'

When we went to the squats, Ig came with. He'd been crashing on our living room floor more often of late and with each trip up from Twyford, he brought with him news of growing countrywide opposition to the vindictive shitsuckers. He'd also taken Sorrell down to Twyford on a couple of occasions, which was fine by me.

Vee liked Ig. She told me that it was obvious that he cared and that he seemed 'very committed.' She said he was 'a sweet and gentle man'. 'I don't want to disappoint you,' I whispered, 'but his favourite film is *Watership Down...*' and we laughed some more at that.

As we span around Mose, I introduced her to other people too, people who knew people that she may once have known. We visited DJ's and backdrop artists and militant cyclists and we sat in ex-boho pads and listened to the new chat.

These afternoons were good for both of us and there was no sign of the nascent mardiness that Vee had demonstrated on her return to Brum. She seemed keen to learn about what was going on. She was attentive, listening in that way of hers that I had come to know and then leaning back, thinking and dangerous, her wit taut between the barb and the interrogative hook. Occasionally it twanged. 'You can sleep when you're dead,' said Madderz, who had been up two nights and was thinking about a third. 'Yeah but if you don't sleep, you don't dream,' said Vee, 'and if you can't dream then what have you got?'

We heard stories about all-nighters that had gone on for three days. A chancer called Dick who'd hooked up with a crew on the free festival circuit. Told them he was a stiltwalker, could do workshops. Wasn't, couldn't. Fell off a pair of two-footers at the Harvest Fayre and broke his wrists. Then there was the techno. Geordie Steve played us Sven Vath and Jeff Mills, Nervous Mark a bootleg of Surgeon, spinning at Brum's own House of God, a night of twisted hardcore that had just started up. There were new parties almost weekly it seemed. I talked Vee through the differences between the Brummie sound and wafty trance and gabber from Rotterdam. She said she liked what she'd heard but she'd got to be in the mood and I said that I was always in the mood, that some DJs just took you there and left you there, in the moment. This is our music, I told her, the sound of a revolution. 'It's difficult to put into words. But then it's not about words, it's about hearing and, and feeling. It's *visceral*, Vee' and she said 'bloody feelings! That's all there is these days!' and so I squeezed her arse and we laughed.

I took her dancing to show her what I meant. We went to a new night at the Coach and Horses on Edward Road in Balsall Heath. The pub was small and aspired to be downmarket. It had one room blacked-out for the party. There were no backdrops, no lights, no dry ice. Just ex-travellers, with tattoo-ed necks, dancing. They looked like American Indians. A war party. The DJ was playing a sound called jungle. Jungle was different. Its beats came out of the speaker stacks in balls of bass and forks of treble. It fused nerve ends and scorched the walls and floor.

And Vee got it, she got it alright. She danced like I had never seen, threw herself into herself, not lost in the music but found. For a moment it wasn't only as though I wasn't there, but as though she had gone somewhere too.

When we had danced, we drank shorts on barstools in the sticky-floored lounge next door.

'What do you reckon, then?' I asked. I wiped my face on the sleeve of my t-shirt. 'You see what I mean now, don't you? It's a good noise, ennit?'

'I used to come here for punk gigs,' said Vee, still out of breath. 'I've seen so many really, really awful bands here it's untrue.'

'Yeah but punk's dead,' I said. 'Seriously. Techno's the new punk. Only we mean it more than they did. A lot of punk was a commercial scam, you must know that Vee, appealing to the lowest common denominator. You know, fuck this, fuck that, disrespect for everything. We're about respect, for each other and the land and...'

'...getting off your head,' said Vee. 'Winding people up, doing what you feel like, not playing by the rules. And the music of course.'

And I told her she was very cynical and she laughed.

If Vee accepted Ig and eased herself by association into the spirographic routine we'd made of our avowedly anti-routine life, she made no such connection to the rest of my acquaintances. In July she moved out of our place and into a room in a shared house on Runcorn Road in Balsall Heath. 'Good choice,' I said, 'Balsall Heath is where it's at,' and she said 'yeah, it's certainly a hell of a lot cheaper than Moseley.' Then she got a temping job, working at the Department of Transport at Five Ways. She needed the money for some new equipment so she could get back to her photography again. I thought nothing of this; some of our lot had been known to take jobs from time to time, so what did it matter if it was for Babylon? Everyone who works, works for Babylon. And anyway, it was only a clerical position. As far as I could tell, it didn't require her to drive a digger or ride a wrecking ball, with a bug in her eye and a whoop on her lips.

Somehow though, Stripe got wind and in true spiky fashion saw an opportunity to lose some influence over would-be friends and allies. Within a week he'd asked Vee to get him details from the personnel files of the engineers that were working at Twyford Down. 'Just for research purposes', he obfuscated, pitifully, just in case he hadn't already taken it a liberty too far in asking her in the first place. Vee said no and Stripe got the hump. According to him, she was now, apparently, 'part of the problem'.

Vee was bewildered by Stripe's aggression and annoyed too. 'I mean he's *such* a twat' she said, a sentiment with which I had previously concurred. But me and Vee were in love and by now I was just giddy enough to know that each of us was too giddy to take any real offence with the other. And so despite my aversion to Stripe's potential sociopathy, I took advantage of Vee's compromised antsiness and defended him. After all, the spat was the perfect opportunity to demonstrate to Vee just how much what we were doing meant to me. 'Granted, petal, he's no shoe-in for personality of the year,' I said, 'but then he's probably just over-excited. I mean how can you not be?'

We'd had some good news from Ig, you see, earlier that week. The protesters that had been nicked at Twyford in May had just had their day in court and had been handed injunctions prohibiting them from returning to the site. The old bill clearly thought that this would put the frighteners on us but they had underestimated our will. As soon as they were released from custody, de-muddied and unbowed, the protesters were back on the Down as part of a five-hundred strong mass obstruction. The government looked on, hapless and shuddered. Two days later, there was an announcement about the Oxleas Wood protest. Seeing the determination of the Twyford defenders, the

Department of Transport had bottled it. The plans for the road through the woodland were abandoned.

'We've done it now,' said Ig, 'they won't like this' and then we were concerned about what they'd need to hatch in response to our growing strength, because the pressure on them was building and it couldn't be long now, could it, I mean the bean-counting cone-hating green-inked Daily Mail brigade would see to that. But then we'd won our first significant victory and there was elation too. If these unenforceable judicial spasms were an example of what they were going to hit us with, how could we lose?

We'd also heard of new protests in Newcastle and Wanstead, South London. In Newcastle, the Cradlewell Bypass was due to go through an area of woodland known as Jesmond Dene. In London they wanted to build an extension to the M11. Put a road through houses, parks. Neither development was necessary. But neither was going to happen either. We wouldn't allow it.

A group of Earth First!-ers called the Flowerpot Tribe had mobilized to protect Jesmond Dene. The focal point of the Wanstead protest was a 200-year-old sweet chestnut that stood on George Green, common land that used to be the centre of a village. Ig said some of our lot were down there building a tree house. They were going to live in it, have it registered as a legitimate address with the Post Office, a move that would give it protection under the law. We would resist the attempts of the developers to stamp all over the wishes of the residents and we would return the area to the people. It would be an enclave, a haven.

'It's about keeping them on their toes, so they don't know what to expect,' said Ig, 'so they don't know what's coming next. If you can fight the system with a bit of wit, it just short-circuits. Creativity, cojones and cheek, that's what we're about.'

He was right of course. And so, with the spikies straining like dogs on string and the fluffies Kum-ba-yah-ing at 80 beats per minute, I said to Vee 'you must be starting to see how much this means to us?' She said 'yes I can, you certainly look good on it' and I said 'thank you' and we kissed and told each other we were in love.

Explaining Mike away was a different story. He'd long since stopped trying to persuade us that he was interested in our politics. It was our move from the front pages of the tabloids to the last-but-one item on Channel Four News that had done it.
One evening Vee had rung the house and Mike had picked up the phone.
'No, sweetie darling sweetie, he's not here. OK. Yes darling, OK. I'll tell him,' he'd said. 'Sweetie.'
Vee had been confused. She'd said to me that she didn't want to have a conversation with the boy but 'he might want to try speaking English anyway.'

What could I say? If it's worth getting mad at someone, it's worth staying mad and despite his best efforts Mike wasn't the sort you could stay mad at. There wasn't enough substance to sustain that level of displeasure. On this occasion I told Vee that it sounded like he was just throwing her a couple of catchphrases from a new sitcom he'd been raving about.
'He's just like me really, well, in some respects anyway. He's just a bit unlucky. He's smart and funny but he hasn't got what I've got. You, to be smart and funny against.'

Vee looked embarrassed about this as she sometimes did when the conversation was about me and her and I said to her, 'there's a lot of Mikes around you know, you can't be angry with them all. Can you? *Vee?*' and she said 'no, no I suppose not' and she shook her head and laughed.

She didn't get Sorrell either which was rather worrying, given that any misunderstanding between them would inevitably result in me copping out big time. 'She's been very nice to me,' said Vee, 'very solicitous. She's always asking me if I want anything but then she looks at me in a very strange way. Almost conspiratorially, Arch. Do you know why she might be looking at me conspiratorially, Arch?' 'Maybe she is just nice,' I said. 'Maybe that's all there is to it.' 'Oh I'm not too sure about that,' said Vee and I wondered if she could tell I was winging it. That very morning Sorrell had said, cheerily enough, over breakfast instant noodles, that I'd 'mess-up with this one just like I had with all the others.' Worse, there had been some very deliberate non-flirting between us of late, the sort that leads to sexual tension. Not that I meant any of it of course, but even so, whatever she was up to I'd have to watch her, that much I knew.

Then Vee got onto the subject of Tom. He'd been couch-surfing again, putting in the odd appearance when Stripe wasn't around. And odd was the word. I hadn't mentioned it to anyone but one morning I'd woken to find two long bladed kitchen knives carefully crossed on the landing outside Stripe's bedroom door. 'Tom?' I said. 'What the fuck?'
'I cast them,' said Tom, 'the knives. They fell in the shape of nauthiz. It's a symbol from the runic alphabet. It signifies my ability to overcome conflict. My ability to survive.'
'Fuck me,' I said, 'it's like Gloria Gaynor is alive and well and swigging white cider' and I braced myself for the usual tirade.

But Tom wasn't there.

This, unsurprisingly, Vee had clocked. 'Your friend,' she asked, 'is he alright? I saw him the other day and he looked in a bit of a bad way.'

'Oh he's alright. That's just Tom. His world ain't never gonna make no sense. And, like I said, it's his achy, breaky hear... he's got woman trouble.'

'Yes, I remember you saying. Anyone you know?'

'Yeah. It's Sorrell. He keeps threatening to do something about it but I'm not too sure what.'

'*The* Sorrell?'

'Yup.'

'The Sorrell who's seeing Stripe?'

'And Tom.'

'And Tom.'

'And Ig.'

'And Ig?' said Vee. 'Do you think so?'

'I don't see why not. In for a penny, y'know?'

'It's very incestuous, Moseley, isn't it?' said Vee.

'Well, yeah. Like you didn't know that already.'

'Oh I knew it Arch, of course I knew it. Don't get me wrong. It's just that it all seems more insular than ever now. All turned in on itself. Don't you think...?'

'Blimey Vee, who died and made you Claire Rayner? You're right though, in a way. I've been thinking that something's got to give with that lot, it's certainly been getting a bit on top, on the quiet. And I'm worried about Tom myself. I was going to try and track him down tomorrow, see if I can't talk some sense into him. You don't mind do you?'

'No, not at all. Actually Arch I can't see you this weekend at all. Something's come up. I need to go to London.'

'Oh. Oh. OK. Something's come up? Is it work?'

'It's a long story...'

'OK, I mean, it's OK, you don't have to tell me if you don't want to, I don't mind. But is it work? I mean...'

'Sort of. Don't worry Arch, it's nothing to worry about. I'll explain when I get back. You have a good weekend. And be gentle with Tom.'

'I will. I love you Vee.'

'Yes, I know, love you too,' she said and we did, we really did.

It is the following weekend and we leave the city on a whim. It is Vee's idea. She tells me she wants to share something with me. She borrows San's motor, an old 2CV and off we chug, through the city centre and into the suburbs of north Birmingham that lie cod-faux grim in Brummie brown and grey. It is the average afternoon of a nondescript Saturday but I am in love. There is no afternoon that is anything less than extraordinary and no weekend for which just any description will do.

Vee doesn't say where we are going. I have some tapes on me, bootlegged sets from the House of God and I say to her

'Don't you want to listen to some techno?'

'No, not today,' says Vee

and I spark up a spliff.

As we drive, I look into the cars that pass by on the other side of the road. In every car, there is a world. I wonder what the people in these worlds are thinking or feel. I wonder if they have had their maybes turn into yeses or have shed tears that have fallen for a thousand miles. I see their images as they flick past, behind glass, and I doubt it. They seem a long way away. They are not like us. We work differently together. Except we don't of course.

Other people *work* together, the people in the cars probably *work* together, on their weekaday weekends in their workaday worlds. I mean it's not their fault, I know that much, it's just that none of these people have got Vee. I've got Vee and we are different, we just *are* together. That is all I need, the affirmative. Our love.

We drive on, along ugly roads. We pass out of the conurbation and into the countryside. It is the wrong kind of countryside. There are entrances to quarries and mineral works. Yellow diggers. Flat-bed lorries are parked up. There are towns, small towns and villages of red brick and sandstone where drizzle should be falling. Burton, Belper, Matlock. Matlock Bath. Birchover. Enemy territory. Places where they haven't heard of the things being done in their name or, more likely, they have and don't care. There is money here. The people aren't Thatcher rich or Thatcher poor, they have Major money, just enough to get by, comfortably, muted, complicit. Just enough to close the mind. They look down their noses at us, for being on the dole, for opting out of the mainstream. For not voting even. They probably vote, from Burton through Birchover, they'll vote every time. But theirs is the real cynicism.

As we drive, Vee doesn't say much. We turn off the main drag and she pulls up in a layby on a loose-surfaced B road. She gestures to a path that rises steeply from a gate in a dry-stone wall and then winds off into a wood. 'I think this is it,' she says, 'yes this is it' and she smiles. I know that she is smiling at a memory, not at me, but she is beautiful when she smiles and it is good to see and I smile too.

Vee unpacks a tent from the boot of the car, goes through the gate and sets off up the path through the wood. I follow. It is soft underfoot with leaf mulch and peaty mud. The trees are oak and birch and sycamore and mountain ash. The wood smells old and new, like the world when you are a child.

It is late afternoon and in the wood the insects are biting. The sun looks warmer than it is. It is iridescent in places, coming through veined leaves in yellows and pinks. I spark up another spliff.

'I used to come here,' says Vee, as if reminding herself of the fact, 'when I was younger...'

'You're not so old now,' I say and then I realise that I don't know how old she is. This realisation is reassuring. We are different, me and Vee. The people in the cars, you see, the cone-headed aliens with green-ink for blood. Now *they'd* know.

The path levels out. Now we are walking on ground that is springy like moss. There are clumps of coarse grass, flat bushes, tiny flowers in yellow and pink. There are silver birch, their trunks just beginning to shiver in the dimming light.

'Where are we?' I ask.

'Stanton Moor, I think it's called.'

'You think it's called? You mean we're lost. Doesn't surprise me. I never had you down as a tree-huggy, outdoorsy-type.'

'A tree hugger?' she says, 'a bloody tree hugger? Listen slat-kee-shoo, I think you'll find that if you can bear to tear yourself away from your beloved techno for just a moment, there's a lot to be said for a bit of quiet time. A bit of reflection. Seems to me there's too much...*chatter* these days.'

'OK,' I say, 'you're the boss.'

'And don't you forget it. You can do a lot worse than keeping that space of yours clear. Filling it with a bit more space, you know?'

Now she is smiling again. This time it is at me.

'Blimey Vee, I can't win can I? Before you came along, with your manipulative feminine wiles, I was more than happy sitting on my arse watching the world go by. Then you tell me I need to put myself about a bit. And then, when I do, you say I'm better off on my arse after all. And what was that 'slat-kee-shoo' all about?'
'I'm sorry?'
'Slat-kee-shoo. What does that mean?'
'My little sweet. Or thereabouts. It's Croat... I think... Well, actually, I know... But enough of your moaning. Let's get this tent up and then we can relax.'

Vee's cameo is over and we stop talking. We have arrived at a circle of stones standing on a patch of closely cropped grass. There are nine stones, each about two foot high. The Nine Ladies says Vee. It is a site of pagan worship, an ancient burial site maybe. There is no sound. No birdsong, nothing. Leaving the tent on the ground, Vee wanders into the circle. She is earnest in reverie. I think about slipping in a gag about wafters or fluffies, possibly some Narnia chat. Then I look at the silver birch. In the gloom their trunks are ethereal, there is no other word for it. So I don't.

We pitch the tent just outside the circle. The quiet is good. When we have pitched the tent we collect kindling and small branches and build a fire. There are more insects. I open a bottle of wine. The circle of stones is serene.
'I know what you mean about filling the peace and quiet with peace and quiet,' I say, 'sometimes at least. Sometimes I feel that way when I'm with you. Or thinking about you. Only sometimes, mind...'
Vee doesn't answer. She doesn't need to. She is looking straight into the heart of the fire and I look at it too. The fire dances and crackles.

When we have drunk the wine, we go for a walk. It is nearly dark. There are trees, dark against the near-dark. There are new old smells, the smoke from wood burning. It is getting colder. We are both shivering but neither of us is feeling the cold. We walk into the wood of silver birch and make love on the springy ground. We are lying on twigs and we laugh. Afterwards I touch Vee's face, stroke her hair. Kiss her eyes. Hold her.

In the dark we are standing holding each other in the silver birch wood, and we are still and the world is going round and everything else is oscillating too, in harmony. Everything is as it should be and we are at the centre of it all and it is ours to know and explore. And I am sad for a moment because I don't want to move or let go. This moment is perfect and I don't want it to end.

We walk slowly back to the circle of stones. The fire has burnt itself to a glow. We stop and look at the embers.

'Let's go this way,' says Vee. 'There's another stone the other side of the circle.'

We walk through the stones. We walk up a slight incline, through more trees and Vee says
'There it is. The King Stone'
and there is a taller stone, luminously pale, looking down over the circle.

'When I was a child,' says Vee, 'all of these stones were real. They all had names, personalities. I can't remember what most of them were called now, but this one, The King Stone, I called her The Queen Stone. I used to imagine being the Queen Stone, looking over the other stones, looking out for the other nine

- 135 -

ladies. There's something about that stone, don't you think? Something... noble? No, that's a bit strong. Full of goodly grace though.'

'Blimey. Let's see. Yup, it's certainly a piece of stone, I mean there's no doubt you've nailed that one...'

'...a graceful piece of stone, if you don't mind ...'

We both laugh.

I say: 'I love you y'know.'

'I know,' says Vee. 'I love you too.'

And then she says: 'Thank you.'

'What for?'

'Like I say. For being here. For letting me indulge myself. For letting me get in touch with a part of myself that I thought I'd never find again. I need this, Arch. I don't know what I'd have done without you.'

We are quiet then. We look up at the sky. It is a clear night and there are countless stars. I look at Vee. She is lost. It seems as though she is counting them. She is funny, beautiful, uniquely intelligent, implacably different. I think back to the day after we first met. The stitching up of me and Ella. She is dangerous too. She keeps me thinking on my pins and makes me feel completely comfortable.

We are good together.

And nothing is ever going to be better than this.

15. The highest experience.

'So, geez,' I said. 'It's been a long time.'
Tom sighed. It was an exhalation that contained multitudes, most of which were rank.
'Has it Arch? Has it really?' he said and I decided to nip my planned procrastination in the bud.

We were sat on the grass in the private park. It was two days after me and Vee had come back from The Nine Ladies. I'd lured him there with the promise of buying some weed and had intended breaking him in gently but I was happy for the excuse to get straight down to it. If Tom's head could take any tranquilliser or stimulant known to man, it was clearly no match for the sexual vicissitudes of the fuck-pot Sorrell, whose carnal unfussiness was rapidly acquiring legendary status within the Village. Procrastination was all very well but I didn't have more than one afternoon spare for this mother of all talks about the birds and the bees.

'Yes Tom. Although time is relative to you not-so-merry prankster sorts, trust me. It's been a long time. But that's not the reason I wanted a spraff. If the truth be told, I'm still worried about you. Vee said she saw you about a week ago, y'see. Down here, sitting on the grass ...'
'...grounded...'
'...out of your box...'
'...I was astral planing, Arch, tapping into my psionic energy...'
'...in your underpants Tom. For fuck's sake. In your pants. So. Let me just ask you one question. How is it going between you and Sorrell? Are you still happy? Is it still some trip?'

Tom sighed again. Pulled on the skunk number, traced a triangle in the air with his hand. Was he conducting a celestial choir? Away with the fairies? Mad?

'Oh yes. Oh yes Arch. It's some trip.'

'Ri-ght,' I said, whoah-ing with difficulty the inclination to indulge my smarts, 'it's just that I see you off on one, like we used to be, sitting in the park, getting banjoed, chasing the higher experience. In that spot where you stop pretending, where you're completely yourself. And that's what love is. But I don't see Sorrell into it in quite the same way. Do you know what I mean? I mean do you think she is? Really?'

'When she's with me, she says it feels like she's coming up, the whole time.'

'Really? It just seems to me that there're too many unanswered questions, you know? Is she being honest with you? Is she still seeing Stripe? Is she *doing right* by you? And love isn't like that, believe me, geez, love just isn't like that. Take it from one who knows. I mean don't get me wrong, me and Vee haven't had it easy. We've been through the fire. When she was away that was all there was, the questions. But if you love each other you come through all of that and you get to the stage where all questions stop, where everything is just right. It's difficult to explain but even if you feel differently about certain things - and even me and Vee feel differently about things sometimes - it doesn't matter, it really doesn't matter.'

'It's like she's coming up, Arch. All the time.'

'No shit,' I said, glancing for my own benefit at where I'd wear a watch, 'let me put it another way. Do you think she knows how much it means to you? Because from what you're saying - at least I think this is what you're saying - she might not know just what she means to you. And she needs to know. You need to show her how you feel. That's the least you can do. The most important thing and the least. Show her that you *mean* it. I waited for Vee, Tom, for two years I waited for Vee. And I was here when she came back. Now you need to show Sorrell that she means as much to you. That she is a part of your highest experience. And if she reacts badly? You'll know it wasn't meant to be.'

Tom looked at me then, as a tortured genius might look at a naif. He put his hands down, pushed himself up to a standing position. Looked impassively at his palms, wiped duck shit onto his jeans and was away.

16. Asking Vee.

Despite what I had said to Tom there was, of course, one aspect of Vee's mysteriousness that I felt comfortable questioning. Her experiences in the former Yugoslavia, her reticence to talk of her time away, the journal or portfolio or whatever it was that she kept under her bed.

By now, I'd looked at the photographs in the big leather book. There were scenes of bucolic grey-stone villages and stone-grey tower blocks, people in the rain, sometimes alone, sometimes in groups looking glum. There were place names handwritten beneath or alongside, alien names, Hambarine, Kozarac, Srcem Do Mira, Stara Rijeka, Tukovi, Brisevo.
In Vee's absence I'd tried to keep up to speed with the situation. Milosevic, there was someone you could hang a hat on. Sarajevo too. But where were these places? Who were these people? And what of her familiarity with the term 'slat-kee-shoo'?

Surprisingly enough, we hadn't spoken about any of this, not yet. She'd previously had opportunities to expand on what I knew of her work and had chosen not to so I'd been very careful not to force the issue. By now though she must see that it wasn't about restricting her head-space or compromising what was special about us. I just felt as if I owed it to her to show an interest. Besides which, she'd never actually explained that trip of hers to London...

We were sitting in our living room, playing chess, when I judged the time was right. Vee had bought a board from the pound shop next to the Prince and I'd started playing again, for the first time since Castlemorton. It was difficult to tell who was winning. It was always difficult to tell who was winning right up until the moment that Vee won.

I said to her: 'Tell me about your work.'
She said: 'What do you mean?'
I said: 'What I say. Tell me everything. I want to know.'
She said: 'Why? Why now? Is this just to put me off my chess?'
I said: 'No. No seriously, it's about time. I mean I love that you're enigmatic and all that, but there's a lot I don't know about you that I'd like to know. And you haven't been very forthcoming.'

Vee sat back then and I saw her eyes dazzle with a fire that, for all of the love we'd since shared, brought to mind the night she'd first put up her poetry-related dukes.

'OK Arch, I'll tell you. I'd love to tell you, actually. The only reason I haven't been very 'forthcoming' is that I haven't felt like talking about my work, not for a while. It's bad over there, Arch, I don't think anyone knows how bad it really is. And besides, I'd expected more people to know about what's going on, or at least to have shown an interest but, to be fair, you've been a bit caught up in yourselves. So it suited us both really, my silence. But no, you're right. I should make an effort too. So. What do you know and what do you want to know?'
'Well, we could start with your agency. I don't think you've ever actually told me what they do...'
'Again, to be fair, you've never asked. But that's alright, I'll tell you now. What I do - what our agency does - is take photographs of situations where there've been potential violations of international law. Some for use as documentary evidence in any future war crimes trials - tho' it seems there's little chance of that at the moment - some to be shown separately, exhibited if you

like, to make more people aware of the situation. We have - we are all involved in - a number of different projects...'

'...I see. And is it the Serbs? Mainly? Doing the violating?'

'...ye-es. But it's a bit more complex than that...'

'...yeah, I know, the Croats were a right bunch of Fascists weren't they? Nazi sympathisers. In the war, the Second World War? I read about that... So. How do you feel about how it's all going? I mean it must have been...I don't know...*traumatic*? But worth it too, I'll bet. You must get a buzz out of feeling you're making a difference. It's the same with me. And the thing is I can see now that everyone can make a difference. That's our credo now Vee, and it's very exciting. Anything is possible. So. What about London? What do you do when you go down to London?'

'London? When I go down to London? Well, the agency is moving the focus of its operations from Croatia to Bosnia and we need to know how the situation is changing on the ground. It's very volatile, very dangerous in fact...'

'...and you go down to London to...'

'...I go down to London to tell them what I know, share contact information...look, Arch? I'm not being funny, but is that what you really want to know? What I do when I go down to London?'

'You make it sound like an ongoing thing...'

'Well, it will be,' said Vee, 'I'm sorry if I didn't tell you that, but it will be.'

And with that she stopped, a long way past the end of our chat. She gestured at the chessboard, leant forward intently.

'Look, hon,' she said, sweetly enough, 'I wasn't being funny when I said that maybe it's for the best. If we don't, you know, go into things. I appreciate your concern but I'm still not sure I'm ready, if it's what I need just now. If you want to know more about what's going on over there, read more, watch more, listen more. And if that isn't enough? Well just read harder, watch harder, listen harder. Yes? It's like poetry, if you like. Remember that? You have to work at it, at finding threads and picking at them, seeing where they go. So. Shall we say that's it for today? And it's still your turn?'

It wasn't until later, much later, that I realised the conversation that afternoon had answered none of my questions and told me nothing more about Vee and what made her who she was. And by then, of course, it was too late. By then, I'd done my worst.

17. Repetitive beats.

The news seeped out over a number of days. The Home Secretary Michael Howard spoke of 'a tidal wave of concern about crime', the need for the countryside to be 'made safer'. And then, just in case these allusions were a bit oblique for the average voter, he name-checked 'New Age Travellers' and 'raves' too.

'These people have even made it onto the Archers,' he said. 'Well I've got some good news for Ambridge. When our new laws are in place, Eddie Grundy won't need to spray manure on his fields to get rid of them.'

The manure crack was apt. The measures he spoke of were part of a new Criminal Justice Bill and they had been scooped from a pick-and-mix shitpot of Daily Mail rhetoric and establishment fear. The government was going to stop obliging councils to provide sites for travellers to park up in. They were going to ban gatherings of two or more people on public or private land that the old bill 'reasonably believed' might cause 'serious disruption'; they were going to create a new offence - 'aggravated trespass' - to deal with transgressors. The pressure on squatters was being ratcheted up, so that people could be evicted after just 24 hours. And, most farcical of all, they wanted to ban the unlicensed playing of music - *ban the playing of music* - that was 'wholly or predominantly characterised by the emission of a succession of repetitive beats'.

It was October 1993 and the wait we'd had since the party at Castlemorton Common was over. This was what they'd thought of. This was their new law. And we were ready for it.

The week after the announcement of the CJB, The Jumping Bean Café opened in the old butcher's shop in Moseley Village. The Jumping Bean was narrow and smoky and furnished with old school tables and chairs. At the back there was an open-plan kitchen serving vegan cheese pizzas, hummus with grated carrot or pasta salad, baked beans on toast and herbal teas. There were no frills in The Jumping Bean and it certainly wasn't a place to eat. It was a place to do business.

On the back wall of the kitchen there was a graff-art mural proclaiming that 'the state will wither as a green rage emerges'. Someone had written 'cars don't dance' in thick black marker. Separating the kitchen from the seating area there was a counter decorated with a cartoon crusty and the words 'from punk and hippy - the Tribes' and 'listening to our own music is not a government-issued privilege - it's a god-given right.' The counter was covered in copies of Squall, a new publication called Do or Die from Brighton, Green magazine and the Earth Island Journal. There were flyers for techno nights and the No M11 campaign, gruesome leaflets from the BUAV. Others were pinned up on a cork noticeboard that had been edged with the Leveller's line I'd first heard on the trip to Castlemorton: *There's only one way of life and that's your own.*

We gathered in the caff most nights in those early weeks, to talk about how we were going to fight the campaign against the CJB. There was Mark and Jackie and Big Dan who ran the caff as a co-op; Ig and me, Little Simon, Ruth, Nick the Hippy, Pritstick, Jen, Stu, sometimes Sorrell, very occasionally a thunderously impatient Stripe. Vee came too, once or twice and I was glad.

Since our conversation about her work, it was almost as if she'd lost interest in ours. I mean, don't get me wrong. I was almost alright with this. After all, we lived grown-up lives, we respected each other's boundaries and made sure that we had room to breathe, yada yada yada...

But the campaign was different. Just as I'd made an effort with her politics, if she was going to be living here, in Moseley, she needed to make more of an effort with mine. Because we weren't playing games. And our politics would come to affect us all.

The vibe of the discussions in the caff was up, chilled, confident. All over the country the sound systems were on the road and fluffy radicalism was growing. Down in Luton, a DIY collective had created a community centre and was throwing parties and doing good works on a housing estate. Despite regular visits from steroid-munching old bill they were succeeding in holding it down. In Wanstead, the children of the local community were being encouraged to adopt the tree house and take part in the protest. When the Department of Transport got wind of a planned tree dressing ceremony, they started to put up a fence; the locals joined forces with the protesters and pulled it down.

At every gathering, Ig emphasised the organic nature of the protests. All organisation of parties or marches or events was to be done by word of mouth. There was to be as little literature produced before the event as possible and as much as we could manage afterwards. It was to be a guerrilla campaign of hit and then run. This would keep the authorities off-balance, make the law unenforceable. 'We need to keep the festival circuit going to stretch the resources of the coppers in the sticks,' he said and everyone in The Jumping Bean was buoyed and Sorrell-like in their enthusiasm at the prospect.

But there were personal tensions too.

Word had just reached us of the comment of a Law Lord, Lord Hoffmann, who'd said that 'civil disobedience on the grounds of conscience is an honourable tradition in this country and those who take part in it may well be vindicated by history.' Ig picked up on this, the irresistibility of our case, the support it was attracting from unlikely quarters. 'With this law they've created a direct action revolution,' he said one night and there was agreement all round until Stripe dived in with: 'Some revolution. What are we going to do? Change their minds by *marching*? We'll change their mind by putting a few of them in hospital, stopping them polluting our air. That's what'll change their minds.'

I'd heard this chat before of course but in Stripe's increasing isolation from the rest of the group there was the Tom-stink of desperation. Ever since Sorrell's trip to Twyford with Ig, Stripe had become more surly and withdrawn than ever, his surge of post-Castlemorton evangelism clapped out. Prior to that he had at least tolerated the idea of fluffies - after all they were still part of 'us' not 'them'. Now, there was no room for them in his world.

The next week there were six of us in the caff, spread thinly on shiny wooden chairs. Stripe had propped himself behind the counter and was making a brew. Ig was talking.
'We need to get people down to Wanstead, to defend the tree,' he said and there was a consensual pooling of offers of lifts and the suggestion of a kitty for fuel. Only Stripe cavilled. There was a pause and then he muttered:
'The bastards won't think twice about burning it down, you do know that don't you? Burning it down and taking the tree house out and everyone who lives there with it.'

At this, Ig frowned. He was rolling a fag.

'What was that?' he said. 'What did you say?'

His voice was measured. The threat in his words was implicit.

'What did I say?' said Stripe. 'You all need to shit or get off the pot. That was what I said.'

Someone giggled, nobody laughed. Stripe glared. He poured his tea down the plughole, threw his mug into the sink and then the words came flying like chips of cheap crockery, 'did you fucking hear me? I've had it with you lot I tell you, all of you. I'm out of here. You're all a bunch of fucking jokers.'

A chair skidded across the room and as Stripe launched towards the door that opened out onto the street, Little Simon pressed himself back against the wall, I moved in behind a table,

'fucking jokers, the lot of you...'

'Yeah?' said Ig from his seat and then as Stripe slammed past, again and loud enough to stop him dead,

'YEAH? Well what are you going to do about it then Stripe? Yeah? What are you going to do, big man?'

Stripe stopped, turned. Slowly. Deliberately. Tilted his head to one side. He was mock-confused then piss-take quizzical, yet all the time you could see it. The violence, running through him like a current. I thought of the ashtray flying across our living room, Smiley Rob telling me he'd done enough damage, the suggestion that he was capable of more, much more. I saw him think about it, give serious consideration to spilling blood on the floor of the vegan caff, to smearing the walls of the caff with Ig's blood. He wanted it so much he was almost imploring. *Please Ig, please. You just try and hold this one down you fluffy shit-out bastard.* No-one else in the room moved. Thought anything about anything. Stripe looked at Ig. Ig looked at Stripe. Ig was immovable.

Stripe waited...

And then Stripe made a noise. Was it a laugh? It was a laugh of sorts, or what passed for a laugh in his deathlessly unfunny world. He was still making the noise as he reached into his pocket, pulled out a lighter and lit Ig's cigarette as Ig sat there and let him, still enjoying himself as he flicked Ig the finger, ducked out onto the street and disappeared. Whatever he was going to do, he wasn't going to be doing it tonight.

I was surprised at the overt nature of the confrontation. Convention-bustingly thick as he was, Stripe must have suspected he was blowing it out of his arse and worse, that everyone in the caff that night had clocked this. Because whatever he said, we were getting things done, all of us. In Highgate, close to the city centre, Pritstick and Jen had been out subverting billboards. It was an old Reclaim the Streets tactic that Ig had told us about that involved doctoring car adverts with slogans. Sometimes they used wallpaper paste and photocopied lettering to look like part of the ad itself, sometimes they just graffed away. The end result was the same. An end to the corporate hijacking of public space.
In Selly Park meanwhile, Nick had painted a bicycle lane onto part of the Bristol Road. The council wouldn't do it, so we did.
Back in Moseley, we had decided to turn our flat into a squat. We'd been on at the landlord about the damp, the curves in the walls for long enough. Why should we be charged rent for somewhere that was unfit to live in? 'You all know someone

round here who's an artist, right?' said Ig. 'Someone whose work is a bit much for the commercial mainstream? Well we'll set up a community art gallery, right here, in a squat, smack in the middle of the village. Show people what real community spirit means.'

Then there was the partying. That was the part of the bill that had most fired our imagination. I mean, trying to ban techno. *Trying to tell us what music we could listen to.* The comedy jokers! The situation was absurd, surreal. A fucking liberty. Those first few weeks we knocked-up backdrops and banners with the help of Mark - who was a scenic artist - and we hung them at parties we threw in a lock-up in Digbeth, at an old garage on the main drag and in the back garden of the Malt Shovel pub in Balsall Heath. We started to spread the word about a party in Victoria Square, in front of the council house in the city centre, for which Ig said he'd try and get the Rinky Dink crew, a bicycle-powered sound system. We decided to challenge the legal nonsense that was "wholly or predominantly characterised by the emission of a succession of repetitive beats'. What was 'a succession'? Three? Four? Wasn't all music predominantly characterised by the beat? We would put together a dance tune that involved a succession of irregular beats, off-beats, beats that weren't repetitive and we would play it at 'unlicensed raves' just to see what would transpire.

And what would transpire? If we showed it was possible to reject unjust laws, change the way that laws were made, show punters a new and better way of doing things. If we could do this *without* violence? That was what we wanted, fluffy and spiky alike. Wasn't it?

But then I suppose the argument between Ig and Stripe wasn't about the relative merits of their approach to activism so much as it was about Sorrell. I'd previously surmised about Ig and Sorrell but only with as much conviction as I'd considered sleeping with the woman myself. Now it was clear that I had been right. Ig and Sorrell were together, in some comedy Moseley form at least. Worse, Ig was, on the sly, ripping the piss out of his less obviously charismatic co-activist. Those 'yeahs' in the caff had been calculated. And however much Stripe thought that he was 'alright' with the situation between his ongoing-erstwhile and all those who sailed in her, he wasn't. Vee had been right about that, I suppose. How everything in Moseley was turned in on itself. Something was going to crack, even as I was unsure what would happen when it did.

Aside from their confrontation, the campaign was producing less than its fair share of the unexpected. At the end of the meetings in The Jumping Bean the group would thin out and some of us would slope on upstairs and carry on in our front room. Mike was always in and although his interest in our activities had been piqued once again by the announcement of the new law, he was still happiest pushing buttons. One evening Ig told us of the different groups that had come together across the country to kill the bill. The Advance Party, a group called Justice? down in Brighton, a loose coalition called the Freedom Network, another that had dubbed the campaign the Velvet Revolution.

After everyone had left Mike said 'blimey, it's like The Life of Brian. You know, '...*splitters*'' and I nearly said something, but although it was such an old line and he was maybe trying to noise me up, it was OK, really it was, because Ig was right, because we were about wit not violence and taking the piss was a part of what we were.

It was also in our flat that Vee made most of her contributions. They were typically pointed, typically apposite. A typical ball-ache. At one discussion, she asked what we thought about the right to silence.

'What's that then?' I said.

'I read something the other day about them wanting to alter the suspect's right to silence, even if they haven't accessed legal representation. It's in the bill. I was wondering what you thought about that.'

'What do I...I mean, we...I mean, what do I think about it?' said Ig. 'It doesn't surprise me. It's all part of the same thing isn't it? There's this state machine lumbering about like a dinosaur in the face of all of this creative energy and it's showing no respect for human rights or freedoms. Too many fair trials and the whole thing grinds to a halt. Look at Oxleas Wood. Why wouldn't they want to stop giving people a fair trial?'

Another time she said 'I know there's not supposed to be a single focus in the campaign but it seems to me the whole thing's a bit uncoordinated. A bit *directionless?*' and Ig looked at me before he answered and then he said 'come on Vee, get up on it, we're not about isms, about thinking in straight lines. Look at what's going on down in Wanstead - because there's no particular focus to what we're doing, there's nothing we can't try. It's not about following a course, it's about getting things done.'

By now I was accustomed to Vee's chat but in Ig's look I saw something of the confusion with which I had first greeted the challenge she brought with her to even the most innocuous of conversations. Just for a moment, my tempered pride in her inquisitorial nature was coloured by embarrassment, an impatience with her implied scepticism or scorn or whatever it was. And as Ig spoke I was reminded of her propensity for over-complicating the issues. For looking too hard. Because you could have too much hard work, whatever Vee said, you could have too much hard work.

One night, I tried to simplify things for her.

'They're fighting a losing battle,' I said, 'whatever they try, they won't be able to stop us. We'll be on the streets, I tell you, thousands of us,' and Vee laughed.

I asked her what she was laughing at and she said 'I suppose I always wondered what it would take to get you lot on the streets, that's all.'

'What do you mean?'

'What I said. I always wondered what it would take to get you lot on the streets. That's all.'

'Yes. Vee. Petal. I heard what you said. But what do you mean?'

'Partying, Arch. That's what's got you on the streets. Of all the things to get fired-up about, that's what's got your goat, that's what the kids of today are angry about. Partying. I just think it's funny that's all.'

She laughed again and I gave her the benefit of the doubt and I laughed too. Until I realised she'd stopped.

'Hang on a minute, Vee,' I said, 'I mean blimey. This is like when you first came back here. Do you know I haven't got a clue whether you're being serious or not?'

'Oh Arch,'

she said and the tone of her voice changed again,

'I've not been sleeping well lately. I'm tired. Can't you just work it out for yourself?'

'Vee...?' I said.

And she frowned and said 'sorry' although I'm not too sure she knew what she was apologising for.

18. The Independent Free Area of Wanstonia.

The next day Ig rang from London with news. He told me about the arrival of many of the defenders of Twyford who'd decamped and were now down in the Smoke, sharing information. They were talking about lock-ons, people padlocking or chaining themselves together or to steel embedded in concrete to delay evictions. They were passing on tactics for mass obstructions, advice on the legality of intentionally confrontational police actions. They were going to squat a row of houses that had been marked for demolition on the route of the road. They were going to break off from the United Kingdom, declare an Independent Free State of Wanstonia, have their own passports and governance. 'It's going to be like a mini-Cristiania,' said Ig and I asked what Cristiania was and he told me it was a community in Copenhagen that was run as an anarchist co-operative. 'There's thousands of people live there, Arch. You should go and see it. Failing that, get yourself down to Wanstonia. See what's going on in the world.'

I hung up and I was elated. Things were going well. I decided to treat myself. I dropped a celebratory little fella. It was pokier than I expected and it knocked me bandy. I went across the road to Nasty Save for a packet of Drum. I saw Tom buying ketchup and two litres of 'Pulse, the Cider with Rhythm'. He was looking OK. He'd been looking better for some time now. He was up to something. I asked him if he'd heard the news.

Later, I went round to Vee's. I didn't normally do 'e' without her. It felt good. She asked me if I'd dropped a pill and I said that I had but that it had nearly worn off. We ate together in her bedroom, pakora from a kebab house on the Ladypool Road. I wasn't hungry and picked at the food and rolled cigarette after unsmoked cigarette. I told her about Wanstead and the Independent Free Area of Wanstonia. She told me that she thought the pakora were a bit greasy and the tomato dip was too sweet. I laughed. I offered her a pill but she said no, she had work the next day. I laughed again and said:

'I love you Vee, I really do. There's me, having a great day, feeling really really up on everything and you're still, oh I don't know, *you*, resolutely *you*, resolutely... *difficult*. I love you so much.'

And Vee said:

'Yeah, there's a reason for that Arch, there's a reason why I'm 'difficult'. I'm difficult because 'it' is difficult, being back here in Moseley is difficult. I came back to chill out, you know, get away from it all, just for a bit. To be with you and have some fun and go to parties and talk about poetry or art or films, or *whatever*. And it's not really working out like that. Is it.'

'I suppose not,' I said. 'I suppose you must keep thinking you're in Disneyland, what with all the Mickey Mouse politics going on around here. With us lot getting het up about partying, I mean what we're doing is about as serious as - what was that thing? From when we were kids? The Mickey Mouse Club, that's it. Do you remember that...?'

'Actually Arch, I know that there's more to it than partying. And some of you lot do too, despite your best efforts to hide it. There's all sorts of implications for civil liberties. It's a serious business. It's a bad law, I've never disputed that. And it's the perfect opportunity to kick against the system, I mean that's important too, of course it is. Everyone needs to kick against the system sometime. God knows, it needs kicking. It's just that sometimes it seems as though that's all there is. The partying and the kicking...'

'Aha,' I said, as more Disney characters came into my head, anarchist cats and ducks and dogs, rocking the boat, doing it for themselves, 'it's funny you should mention that...'

'...and before you say anything else,' said Vee, 'I'm not sure the best time to have this discussion is when you've dropped a pill.'

OK, OK, now that was a fair cop. Classic Vee. Besides, she'd said *I've never disputed that* and it was true and I was happy with this. For all her mithering she was on my side, of course she was. I had been wrong to doubt her commitment, not that I was, not really, I had just been knocked bandy by the excitement of the campaign. And the ecstasy. I should tell her that. In that order. She'd like it. It was funny.

We drank more wine and then we made love, sort of. I remember thinking it was as though she had just taken off a pair of pyjamas, bless her. I couldn't get it out of my head that she had just taken off a pair of pyjamas, like some Burton Belper type would have to before they made love, and I stayed up with this thought as she slept, laughing to myself as the residual effects of the 'e' wore off in the stillness and it wasn't until the next morning when I saw she had left for work that I realised that it wasn't very funny at all.

19. What was I to think?

There were many such comedic misunderstandings during those wintery autumnal weeks. The stillnesses in which we were most complete had become fewer, the ifs and maybes had reappeared. The questions had begun again.

Just what did Vee want from me? What had she meant about being wrong to question the space between me and the serious and meaningful? Why was her enthusiasm for the Velvet Revolution so guarded? Was she grafting, trying to make sense of things? Or just taking the piss?

At the time, I didn't care to ask these questions. I didn't care to think about us, not beyond the obvious anyway. As far as I was concerned the questions had been answered. She was what I wanted, I was what she wanted, we were meant to be. What was left to ask?

I mean I wasn't daft. I knew we were in the throes of a comedown from the great yes, so any off-key moments or doubts in our relationship were to be expected. But it wasn't that we were any less in love or that our love was no longer different to the love that other people knew. It couldn't be. This was me and Vee, after all. We had the Nine Ladies. We were special. Even after everything that we had been through we were together, giving each other head-space maybe, acknowledging that we each had our own ways of doing things, *respecting* our own ways of doing things, but getting on with it, loving each other. That was what mattered. Not the differences in the in-between.

There would be differences, of course. I would always be more relaxed, laid back, light-hearted. Vee would always be more intense. Jesus, she could be intense. 'It can't go on like this,' she'd repeat, regularly, apropos of the latest angle on the great Moseley love rhombus, 'it's going to go wrong.' But despite this chat the differences didn't matter. As long as we had each other, the rest could look after itself. Surely the rest could look after itself?

For a while it seemed as though it would. In fact, there was only one occasion when it seemed as though it may not. I think back sometimes to that December Thursday, shortly after I'd begun the careen through the festive blaze...

That afternoon I'd heard from Mickey the Sleeves that there was going to be a squat-warming party in the old bank in Highgate. He wasn't sure who was playing but someone had tatted a projector, Bob was bringing his glitterball and it sounded like a go-er.

I rang Vee at work and suggested we went. I thought it would do her good. Vee had been really under it at work that week and we'd not seen each other since Monday. She'd been sleeping more badly than usual too and had taken to nipping out for a streetlit stroll around the Village or an alley-scanning stride through the ghetto. I was glad to be in a position to suggest some practical assistance.

On this occasion she didn't answer straight away. I could hear her, in her Babylonian bubble, silent on the end of the phone. I could see her too, regarding her options with the enthusiasm of a hippy in a burger bar. After what seemed like more seconds than were strictly necessary she said that she couldn't come because she had to get up early for work the next day.

I tried a line.

'Yeah, but Vee, it'll do you good. Just think of it as doing your bit for a better world.'
This time there was no pause and Vee said 'yeah, take the piss Arch, it's what you do' and the tone of her voice was flat and I suppose I must have just missed the threat in the deadpan.
'I was being ironic Vee,' I said, 'everything's ironic now, hadn't you noticed? Oh yes. And it's only going to get more ironic from here on in,' and then there was no way I could have missed what followed.
'I'd noticed,' said Vee. 'And how exactly did that happen? When, exactly, did this bull*shit* come about?'

I was shocked. Was this our first real argument? I knew that such milestones were of fatuous significance only, but even so. It was certainly the first time that we'd had words that were more deeply bitter than the pith of our everyday banter. I briefly considered meeting her plosive enquiry with an equally violent response. Then I bailed and said sorry. Vee regained her equilibrium and for a few days it seemed as though we'd ridden the incident out.

But then that was just before my politics and the rest of it began to demand more close attention. Just before everything began to come apart and then came apart, bathetically, like Castlemorton in reverse.

20. 'This is where it starts.'

On December 7, they hit Wanstead with the riot cops and everything went crazy. They came at five in the morning in the middle of a storm from the pages of the Bible. Before the bailiffs could gain access to the tree, four hundred protesters had to be moved from the old village green. The protest was peaceful and the coppers were scum. Non-thinking and violent and defeated like thugs, they bullied, punched and kicked their way through the fluffies, the locals, the schoolchildren who'd come out to obstruct the state. It wasn't until noon the next day that they'd managed to cut through the lock-ons encircling the tree and put a digger in place. It took them fully eight hours to bring down the tree house and topple the sweet chestnut tree.

That afternoon, Ig spoke to me over the phone. He was speaking from a pub. He'd had a tot. This wasn't Ig the immovable, this was the Ig from the Clifton.

'I'll never forget it Arch, seeing that tree come down. This is the start of it, believe me. This is where it starts. This is the missing link between the greens and reclaiming the streets, between the city and the country, between the Tribes and the straights. The people are on the move, I tell you. The kids were out with us this morning and the punters who live here as well, an old woman who'd lived next to the green since back in the day. And do you know what Arch? Do you know what we did? This one's for you, old son. We danced. They couldn't stop us dancing, Arch. *They couldn't stop us dancing.*'

The next day Ig came back to Brum. He was calm again but unconvincingly so. He told us that the Freedom Network were bringing together a 'summer of fun' in opposition to the bill. The centrepiece was going to be a national demo, in London, in

July. 'It's going to be bigger than the poll tax,' he said, 'bigger than Castlemorton.' He told us he'd told the M11 lot about our squat cum gallery in the centre of Moseley village and that similar action was being taken all over the country.

'Do you know what you've got to do,' he asked, 'to set the thing up?'

'Stop paying rent?' said Mike.

'Well yeah, but if we're going to do it properly we've got to say why. Officially claim squatter's rights.'

'And stop paying rent.'

'All in good time my little bread head, all in good time. So. Do you know whose name the electricity is in? And the water?'

'Electricity's in mine,' I said. 'Don't know about the water. Might be Stripe's. Sorrell?'

'Do you think he tells me anything, yeah?'

'OK, well if he ever shows up again we'll go over it with him as well,' said Ig. 'The point is, we can stop paying them as well. Whatever happens, once we're officially a squat, we've got a right to water and power. The law's a bit hazy at the moment but if you write to them Arch, I'll go over what you've got to say tomorrow. Anyone else wondering about anything?'

'Not me,' said Sorrell.

'When can we stop paying rent?' said Mike.

The next morning I wrote to our landlord. We were now officially a squat. That would serve the rob-dog right. Why should he be allowed to rent out a place that was barely habitable? I was now officially a squatter. It felt as though I was different. I felt good. It felt as though we were making a difference. I felt proud. Me and Mike and Sorrell kept our own rooms, me and Sorrell on the first floor, Mike on the second.

Next to Mike's was a spare room, for visitors or anyone who needed a place for the night. There was still no sign of Stripe.

That afternoon and the next day, we scoured the Village for talented Moseley heads. We put pictures on the walls of the hall, liberated from bedsit retrospectives. There were caricatures of local punters from Wee Jason, oil-pastelled Gothic gloom from Jimmy Wibble, fantasy landscapes from Jo Garvey. Some of it looked accomplished, some not. It didn't matter. This wasn't about rigid definitions of what constituted 'art'. Why should art just be what you could see in the Ikon Gallery? What about what we said was art? This was about creative energy. And besides. Art was just a part of it. The space was ours and we would use it as we wanted. We'd put on parties, cook big pots of communal food. We'd show short films from local filmmakers, animations from animators, just like The Exploding Cinema, working out of Brixton's Cooltan squat down the Smoke. We would be somewhere people could come if they wanted a meal or needed a place to stay. It would take time - until the New Year perhaps - but we would become a community resource.

The day after that, Tom moved back in. He seemed to have saned-up a bit since Stripe's flounce-out of The Jumping Bean and subsequent disappearing act. True, he'd managed to get hold of an advance copy of something called Vurt, a new novel that looked a bit risky for a man in his positions, but he had taken to wearing trousers when he was out of the house and had stopped delivering would-be gnomic one-liners in response to offers of cups of tea.

It was good to have him back. I realised I'd missed him.

'I've been thinking about what you said,' he said. 'About Sorrell. And I've got an idea.'

'Shit geez, not an idea. Do you remember that last idea you had? About investing in those four hundred microdots from Shifty Phil, up the Traf?'

'Shifnal Phil, Arch, Shifnal Phil. He was from Telford. And I'm not talking about that sort of idea. I've decided I'm going to show her. I'm going to show her that what this means to me. That it is part of the highest experience.'

'You're not going to get your cock out again are you? You do remember what we said about that ...'

'Moron.'

'No, seriously geez, if you've thought it through I think that's great. I'd just say one thing, by way of warning. Don't be fucking with Stripe. I mean he may be slow but he's desperate. And he can be pretty dangerous, too...'

'Pretty dangerous eh? Yeah, yeah, Sorrell's told me all about his juvenile little tendencies. But don't think for one minute that I haven't got the measure of Stripe.'

Of Ig and his potential for Sorrell-related cosmic mayhem, Tom said only that he wasn't 'a convincing rival' and that he 'bore him no ill will'. Bore him no ill will, eh. Jesus. Saner he might be but he'd gone from seeking conversations with god to nicking the old boy's chat. Just as I was beginning to get my head around the implications of his forthcoming idiot-fest with Stripe, the man himself paid a visit to the squat.

He looked as though he'd been having a particularly successful time of it since I last saw him. In the dodging of soap, in any case. I thought back to Tom and his struggle with the thistle. Felt bad, momentarily, for the pair of them.

'Sorrell here?' Stripe asked, not managing to be matter-of-fact about it.

'She'll be back in a minute,' I said and then wished I hadn't, 'listen, mate...'

'Don't you fucking 'mate' me,' he said and I left him to it.

A couple of days later, Sorrell accosted me in the Traf. It was the afternoon of a day I'd started to write off to a Christmas Special Offer on shorts. The pub was quiet. I was standing at the bar in the lounge when she appeared at my elbow.

She looked good. For once, uncomplicatedly good. There was something about her that, even then, after all of my resentment at her attempts to get under my skin, I felt drawn to. Like when you are drawn to a mirror after a party, even though you know you'll be alarmed by what you see. I looked her straight in her nonny-no eye, cocked her my head.

'Can you buy me a drink, yeah?'

'Seeing as you asked so nicely.'

'Arch? Yeah? I'm not in the mood.'

We sat down in a corner. I was on Grants Vodka and Sorrell was being gratuitously over-familiar with a cheap double gin and tonic.

'What gives then, my little ball of mendacious delight?'

'It's Stripe. I'm going to finish with him. I saw him last night and he threatened me. About Ig.'

'Not Tom?'

'Jesus, no, not Tom. He doesn't know about Tom. But he's too much, Arch. Too intense. He's going to do something stupid, I know.'

'Tom?'

'Stripe.'

'Well I hate to say it,' I said 'but then we've always been honest with each other, at least up to a point. You've had this coming, this fuck-up. You can't spend your life flitting from one person to the next and then be surprised when it all turns in on itself. You've got to start seeing the bigger picture.'

'Flipping heck Arch yeah, who died and made you Claire Rayner?'

Sorrell said that she was leaving Moseley in the New Year. She said that she was going down to Glastonbury to travel with a tribe of Druids. Become a Bard, do some poetry. I wanted to tell her that she shouldn't because she belonged in Moseley but she seemed almost sad and I almost felt for her and I couldn't. After she'd finished her second double she left the boozer and I was sorry that she'd gone.

And then Ig broke his leg. It was the day before New Year's Eve. He was crossing the road for a bag of chips from the newly christened 'Mike's Kitchen' when a car hit him as it slewed along the slip road in front of the Fighting Cocks, where people used to stand outside the pub and party. He was thrown onto the bonnet and into the road. He was in hospital overnight and then sent back to us with his leg in plaster. Mike tried a line - 'so it's true - white men can't jump - out of the way at least' and said that it was ironic, what with Ig's aversion to car culture, that he'd been knocked over.

He was right about that, of course. It wasn't funny though. Although Ig was his usual self, full of excitable phlegm, the accident was bad timing. We had work to do. The campaign may have been organic but some of us were better at being organic than others. Ig was our link to London and Brighton and the rest of the country. He knew people, people outside Moseley.

And then there was Stripe. Stoating about, threatening hippies. Stripe still had his key to the squat. A two-legged Ig had managed to face him down. I didn't fancy anyone else's chances.

The night he came back from the hospital, Ig took Stripe's bed. Sorrell, distracted, rueful, didn't seem particularly welcoming but then what was she to do? And then Tom, doing an amateurish job of hiding his excitement with his idea, began to whistle, tunelessly, unnervingly and to look like Bambi consumed by cunning...

21. Old skool.

It is the late afternoon of New Year's Eve. Moseley is bright around the edges with fairy lights and expectation. Dave from Brighton and his girlfriend Sara are upstairs, Mike, me and Tom are in the living room of our squat. Is it our squat? Is it just a squat? I don't know. They haven't written the book on that one yet. They haven't written the book on any of it yet.

Me and Tom are pacing up and down. We have started early. We have just scarfed a line of billy. Now we are smoking bifters and sharing a quarter of finest English brandy.

I have spent most of the day helping to rig up backdrops and lights in The Jumping Bean. There is a party there later on. Tom has said that he will accompany me. I have warned him there will be dancing and merriment but he has said he will come anyway.

In the living room, Mike is wearing a t-shirt that says 'Only Users Lose Drugs.' He is telling me what his resolutions are. He is going to buy one of those cell phones. It'll be great, he says. I'll be able to keep all of my conversations private. Ah yes, I say, but who's told you you've got anything to say that anyone else wants to hear in the first place? Touche Arch, says Mike, very droll.

I ask him what he is doing tonight.
'I don't know yet,' he says. 'I haven't decided. Don't try and pin me down, maan, I'm a free spirit. I think I'm just going to sit here and wait for the night to come to me.'
'Very poetic,' says Tom. He offers Mike the brandy and says 'Happy New Year geez.'

~~~

Just before we set off, I cross to the tape player in the corner of the room.

'Do you mind if I... Mike? Yes, here we go. Just listen to this. It's Surgeon playing at the House of God. Hang on, hang on...here it comes...
Just listen to that! *Oh fuck yes. Come on...!*'

And Tom and I leave and Surgeon is with us...

~

It is five in the afternoon. It is headily cold. The air is damp and there is the blat blat fssss of fireworks from down in the ghetto. They are up to something down there, you don't need to worry about that. And they know how to party.

We are going visiting. Tom does not do much business these days but this is New Year's Eve and his merchandise is in demand. He is wearing a suit. His suit is from the PDSA in Kings Heath. It is tweed. The sleeves of the jacket are too short for his arms and the trousers too short for his legs. Tom can look like a jakie. In his suit he looks like a jakie who is down on his luck. I do not mind this. I am thinking about old times.

I am seeing Vee later on. She is coming to the party at The Jumping Bean. But at the moment it is this Tommysesh I am most looking forward to. For all that I've changed these last months, for all that I have learned about love and politics, there are still nights when the sacrament of getting off your head is all that counts. And this is one of them. This is New Year's Eve. This is the big one.

As we walk up Woodbridge Road smoking a skunk number, Tom is chipper. We talk about our pills.

'Something else, Arch,' he says. 'Whatever I get up to, I don't want you to worry about me.'

'You riling Stripe? Genius boy. Because I'd watch out if you are...'

'Not at all, not at all. And don't you worry about Stripe. I know Sorrell, what she needs. And as far as Stripe's concerned, I'm going to take care of business.'

'Take care of business?'

'Take care of business.'

'Jesus. Tom?'

'Never better geez, never better.'

Tom's first drop is a new punter, name of Seamus. Tom heard about him through Big Dave last night, rang him this afternoon. He wants a dozen pills. He lives in one of a terrace of huge shared houses on Forest Road. As we arrive we have just finished the spliff. My nose is running with the cold. I feel very good.

The drive in front of the houses is old gravel, mud and pebbles. The houses are grand and shabby. Me and Tom have been to parties here, back in the day. There are fluted stone columns, a row of large windows covered with patchworks of sheets and ethnic throws. Away from the street lights it is now dark. From the gaps in the coverings there is low orange light, pale yellow light, a red light. The first porch we come to has six bells. Tom rings one and nobody answers. He rings another and the front door is opened by a geezer called Richard. He has stockinged feet.

'Tom. Arch. How's it going?'

Tom is quiet.

'Sorted geez,' I say. 'What you up to tonight? You going to The Jumping Bean?'

'Yes-aye.'

'Listen,' I say, 'do you know a geezer called Seamus? He said he lived here. He wants something.'

'Yeah, I know him. Look, come in, come in. He's just nipped out to Maini's for some alcohol. He won't be long. You can come in and wait if you like.'

We go into a wide hallway. It is dimly lit but my senses are fizzing with the chems. There is the smell of incense in the cold air of the hallway. Spicy, musky, cinnamon. The smell of old Mose. There are bicycles up against the wall. One of them has no front wheel. The floor is tiled. The tiles are worn down, dipped in the middle, cracked and chipped. There is a reedy rush mat, wet at the edges.

'That's Seamus's there,' says Rich. There is a door off the hall that is slightly ajar. As Rich shuffles past, heading for another room at the back of the house, he pauses.

'It'd probably be alright if you wanted to wait in there, as it goes. He won't be long and he's an OK geezer. He never locks his door if he's just popped out...'

I push the door, walk into Seamus's room. It is a big high-ceilinged bedsit cum studio flat. It smells of damp. It is lit with a forty-watt bulb. It is too gloomy for shadows. There is a bookcase against one of the walls, pink and purple silks hanging like curtains in the large bay window. There are two sofas in the middle of the room, around a low table inlaid with squares of thick glass. There is a chessboard on the table. I go to the bookcase, Tom sits on a sofa and starts to skin up. The books on the bookcase are Arthur C Clarke, Isaac Asimov, Philip K Dick.

'We should play chess again,' says Tom, from the sofa in the middle of the room, 'one of the days.'
I turn to look at him but I can't see his face.

I say 'Yeah. I think I owe your sorry ass a whupping. You should have a look at some these books by the way. Looks like the kind of nonsense you'd appreciate...'
There is a book there by Philip K Dick called *Confessions of a Crap Artist*. The back cover says that it is about a man who collects silly ideas and is very badly equipped for real life.
'This one looks like you,' I say as I read. 'Have you read it...?'

I hear the sound of the sofa being shoved back and the table scraping and I turn round with the book in my hand to give to Tom.

I see Tom running at the bay window.

I wonder why he is running. Do I know why he is running?

Tom runs. I know why he is running.

I wonder about the silk covering the window. I think that if his limbs get tangled in the silk the glass will stab through his body. Then Tom is in the bay and without breaking stride he throws himself into the air. For a moment he is framed, tightly wound, disappearing into the gloom...
...and then the silk is pulled down and the window is a splintered gap into the night and Tom is gone into the dark outside.

It has taken endless seconds. They are still passing. I cross to the window and look out through the broken glass. Tom has gone. He must have picked himself up. He must be OK. I wonder why he didn't look like a desperate man, why he didn't flail. I notice it has started to rain. There is cold air in the room. It is quiet.

Then Rich slides into the room, whites of eyes and stockinged feet. He *slides*. He is no longer shuffly.
'What the fuck was that?' he says.
'It's alright,' I say. 'He jumped out of the window but he must be alright because he's walked away.'
'He's not the only one,' says Rich. 'If you think I'm hanging around for Seamus to come back and find his window's mysteriously disappeared on the coldest night of the fucking year you're even more of a yoyo than your fucking mate. Does Seamus know where you live?'
'No.'
'I'd keep it that way if I were you, old son.'

I pick up the spliff that Tom has rolled, spark it up, feel the smoke curling into my lungs.

'Just getting rid of the evidence,' I say, old-skool comedy-joking visiting-style. And then the seconds rush to nothing with the hit of the smoke and I am back in the moment, the accelerated moment as Rich says

'Yeah. Listen, no offence like, but you couldn't do me a favour could you?'
'What's that?'
'Just fuck off out of it?'

~

I go visiting, on my own. I am on the charge. You'll never guess what? I say, giving it large, teeth-grinding, bug-eyed, loquacious.

Nobody cares about Tom, not really, but it is a good night for it, the chat and the charge.

~

On my way home, striding past the Traf. Pounding. Early evening. Alive in the night. Stripe is there. Standing in the light from a lamppost, the rain falling as stars. He is on his own. He looks like he is dancing. I cross the road, keep to the dark. I pass him, see that he isn't dancing. He's boxing raindrops, fighting the rain.

~

Back at the squat, Mike calls to me as I go up the stairs. 'Arch? Geez?'

He sounds like he is waiting for something. I double triple up the last few steps and fly onto the landing. I am bouncing. Maybe it is me he is waiting for, my chat. I'll tell him about Tom. He'll find it funny. As I slam open the door he moves around behind the sofa in the middle of the room. 'You'll never guess wh...' I start and then I see his face. His mouth is swollen. One of his eyes is nearly closed. There is a cut on his forehead.

'Stripe's been here,' he says, 'he asked me if I'd seen Sorrell. I said 'no' and then he said I was lying and then I said I wasn't, it's just nothing to do with me and it isn't is it? I mean why would I want to get involved, it's got nothing to do with me has it? Arch? I mean it's not my fault is it, if they can't keep themselves under control. None of it is my fault. And then he's gone mad, he's gone all Taran-fuckin-tino on my ass. He's a turbo-nutter I tell you, a turbo-nutter.'

'Blimey,' I say. 'You coming out?'

But Mike just looks past me at the door as he stands and grips the sofa, as he keeps the sofa between him and the door and the night.

~

I go downstairs to The Jumping Bean. I dance. I am charging. Ecstatic. It is a top party. The walls of the caff are wet with sweat. There must be fifty, eighty, a hundred people in there. I see Finula, Big Dan, Big Dave, Jude, Mickey the Sleeves. And was that Wee Jase? All Moseley is there. Our Balsall Heath too. Ig is there. On crutches. In the middle of the floor. He is giving it 'This is our year Arch, this is our fucking year!' and who is going to argue with that? This year we will take to the streets, reclaim the streets. This year things will change. We will change them. Oh yes. *This year there will be a Velvet Revolution!* I tell more people about Tom. I am unsure why or where the boy is now but all such doubt is lost in the moment and the beat. The beat. *The beat. Jesus* the party sounds good. And the look of it too. The lights are picking out hands in the air above the mass of bodies. This is what it is all about. A mass of individuals. Together. United in difference. The shared experience of now. These are the moments we wait for. It doesn't get any better than this. Life. Tribes. Moseley punters. Community. Together. Dancing. Sacramental. A rite. Through history. A *right. Since time.*

Then out the back, by the big metal rubbish bins. There is an open-sided marquee. It is cool under here. Time for a breather from the dance floor. I talk to Vee in the mist drizzle, the misty night air. I tell her about Surgeon and what I've dropped that night and how it's a big one alright and she asks whether I'm worried about Tom and I say no, not really, he got up and walked away didn't he, it's just old skool, innit?

Later. Vee says she'd like to talk to me about something. Upstairs. I tell her not now, Vee, not tonight. I've had it up to here, tonight, with the serious and meaningful. She says very funny Arch, Very Fucking Droll.

Vee goes home. I dance. People drift off. I help to de-rig the party. Then dance. Drift off.

At noon I go to sleep.

~

I am dreaming. Am I awake? I hear banging. It is very loud. It thuds into my overworked heart. I wake up. It is dark. I go back to sleep. Abyss deep.

~

Then my bedroom door is smashed open,
what the fuck?
a voice, out of the black
'ARCH? ARCH!'
Stripe?
'WAKE UP!'
I roll off my mattress onto the floor.

'DOWNSTAIRS! GET UP! NOW!' says the voice,
and there are crutches,
stabbing,
Ig?
'NOW ARCH, NOW!'
it is Ig.
But what does he mean?

I lurch to my feet through the holes in my jeans eyes smarting in pain.

There is pain in my lower back. I am awake too quickly with an hour's sleep? with not enough sleep. There is smoke I smell smoke.

From the kitchen?

'FIRE! THERE'S A FIRE!'

What?

Ig pivots onto our landing Mike is already there, heading past him back towards me, away from the stairs, there is smoke coming from the stairs. It is thick and grey. Mike has a Tom-nuts look in his eye. He is humming a tune. To a TV show? *Dum dum dum...* what the fuck? It's only *London's Burning...wuh-wuh-wuh-wuh, w'w'wuh...* He is quickly past me and into my bedroom. I hear the door locking. Now what do I do? *What the fuck do I do?*

'IS ANYONE ON THE TOP FLOOR?' says Ig. 'DID ANYONE STOP HERE LAST NIGHT?'

I'm not sure-don't think so-not sure-can't think-don't know. Dave? Sara? Jo may have crashed and Andy or Sue and what about Tony from Brixton? I shrug shake my head. Smoke is coming from downstairs. There's a fire. By the front door. Smoke stings my eyes, catches in my throat. We need to get out. We need to get out.

'ARCH? GO UPSTAIRS. QUICK. CHECK UPSTAIRS OUT. MAKE SURE THERE'S NO-ONE THERE.'

'Upstairs?'

'I'LL SORT THE FIRE.'

Shit.

'Yeah.'

'Dum dum dum...'

Fuck.

'I'll check.'
'...wuh-wuh-wuh-wuh ...'
Shitfuck.
'...w'w'wuh...'
I'll check...

~

And then...as I stood on the landing outside my bedroom, with the squat burning, Ig shouting, smoke thickening, Mike freaking-on-the-sly, even as I knew that someone had to go upstairs to check out the other rooms, to make sure that no-one was asleep up there, to make sure that there would be no-one dead in their beds, eaten alive SaraDave by the flames, I found myself unable to move.

It was peculiar this paralysis. I'd like to think it was the nearness of death that had jelly-limbed me, the thought of burning alive that had flattened me against the wall. Or that I had been made helpless by piss-taking time as it blurred back and forth, sped up or slowed-down before stopping. But time wasn't playing games and although death was near it wasn't near enough to move me or stop me from moving.

No, it was the onrushing of a just-awake consciousness that did for me. An irresistible chaos of tunes and projections and images, taking me so far and then shorting, all of them shorting.
I heard techno from Surgeon - 'London's Burning, London's Burning' -
'ARCH! CHECK UPSTAIRS! ARCH CHECK UPSTAIRS!' - 'wuh wuh wuh wuh, wuh wuh wuh wuh'.
I nearly cried out loud at the irony of inhaling too much smoke, at the fire brigade finding my ready-rolleds - Now They'd Do Something About The Cones! I saw Tom and hugged myself as he jumped out of Dave's window, saw him watching as me and Ig took flight too and landed, clear of the fire, a jam-jar mess on the pavement in front of the squat.

There was Vee taking photos of bodies in Moseley, a memorial party - Geraldine meeting Cosmo - the back room of the Coach and Horses, the road through Burton Belper, the Spiral Tribe at Castlemorton, Mike Morris reading the news...

And none of it was any use. Try as I did to find something, anything, to hang my hat on, to get me thinking more clearly and doing, get me off the wall and up the stairs and then somehow, somehow out of the squat before I was fried - the not-bad, nearly damaged and burned alive - still I was standing, moved yes, but unmoving...

~

Then I hear Ig. Through the smoke. From a long way away.

'It's alright,' he says from the other end of the landing, 'Arch? It's alright.' I can see him in the smoke. He is waving his crutched arms and peering down the stairs, through the smoke, at where the smoke is coming from. But the smoke is getting thinner. It smells strong but it is not thick. This is a good sign. The smoke is not thick.
'I think it might have gone out,' says Ig.

I move slowly down the landing, leaning against the wall. I hear nothing from my bedroom. Mike has stopped humming. He unlocks my bedroom door. 'Geez?' I say, 'geez' he says. The three of us gather at the top of the stairs. We look down. Grey petals are dissolving in the stairwell. There is the smell of smoke. There is no smoke. There is no heat. We can't see any flames.

I tread carefully down to the small landing where the stairs go round a corner. There are two or three charred copies of the Yellow Pages lying on the floor inside the door.

'Fuck,' I say. 'It looks like it was started deliberately.'

'No shit,' says Ig.

Then the front door is unlocked and pushed open. The pile of blackened paper scrapes along the floor and then crushes against the wall. It is Sorrell. She looks shaken. There is a policewoman standing in the alley outside. Sorrell says 'I just got home and the police were here. They said someone rang them, said they saw smoke. What's going on Arch? Is Ig about?'

I say 'I don't know what's going on. There's been a fire, that's all I know.'

Two firemen appear. They take a look at the front door, the mess on the floor and push past me and Mike on the stairwell. The policewoman has been joined by a policeman.

'Do you live here sir?' says the policeman. 'Do you mind if we ask you a few questions?'

One of the firemen walks behind Ig as he crabs down the stairs. The four of us follow the copper to a patrol car. They sit us, in turn, in the back. Ask us, in turn, if we have any idea who might be responsible. If we know anyone who might have a grudge against us.

We wait on the pavement until we have all been questioned. It is cold and our bones are chilled. Then we go back inside.

'Not too sure I'm a big fan of this squatting lark,' says Mike.

'What did you say?' says Ig to Sorrell, 'to the old bill?'

'What do you think?' says Sorrell, 'yeah? I mean what am I going to say? I tell you the man's too much.'

'The man's a wanker,' says Ig. 'Funny thing is though, I could have sworn I heard someone knocking the door. Just before I noticed the smoke. I mean I know the geezer's a loser but that's a bit funny, isn't it? Knocking the door to let us know he's trying to burn us out?'

'Yeah,' says Sorrell, 'fucking hilarious.'

22. Boarded-up.

The night of the fire belonged to Moseley from the moment Ruth saw the fire engine on the pavement outside the squat. The days that followed hurried by in frenetic and politicised re-imaginings of what had happened. The fire had been started variously by Stripe, our landlord, or an undercover outfit working on behalf of Group Four Security and the Department of Transport. Our roles too, were a matter for conjecture. Ig had put out the flames, so most versions had it, just as they had begun to blacken the flaky paintwork of our staircase. The rest of us had to make do with bit parts in keeping with the pieces of us Moseley already owned. Had Sorrell been playing with indoor fireworks? asked Eric the Dread; was it true Arch, that you slept through the whole thing? I heard you'd been skinning up for Ig as he hoyed the buckets of water... This latter suggestion was at least welcome, being both a validation, of sorts, and a distraction from the troublesome reality in which I was being bruised and trying to hide my bruises.

After the fire it all happened so quickly you see, too quickly I thought, yet irresistibly too, like love or the end of love...

That evening, Vee rang me and said she had something to tell me. I said 'me too, you'll never believe it.' Round at hers I asked her what she wanted to say and she said 'you go first' and I told her that we'd had a fire. She asked if anyone was hurt and I told her some of the story and that 'no, we were lucky, it was a real amateur job, someone playing with matches. But that's Stripe for you, I suppose.'
She said 'how do you know it was Stripe?' and I thought about it and decided to stay loyal to Tom. I said 'come *on*, even the coppers have worked out that it's Stripe.'

When I said this she frowned and said 'that's interesting'. I asked what she meant and she said 'do you know what, ever since I've been back I've not quite been able to put my finger on what's wrong, and now you've gone and nailed it, just there. It's about the way you connect with the outside world.'

'What do you mean what's wrong? Is there something wrong? Do you mean with us?'

'No Arch, not with us. Right and wrong is about more than just me and you. But there it is again, since you mention it.'

'There what is? What are you saying? Is this what you asked me over for? Because if it is I'm none the wiser...'

'What? Oh. No. That was something different. You know I've been planning to go back to Croatia? Well, I've got something to tell you. I've been sorting out when the best time will be. And I'm going to leave in about a month.'

'A month? Ohhh. OK.'

'Is that it?'

'Is that what?'

'Just 'OK'. Is that it?'

'Why not? I knew you were thinking about it. And you are your own woman. I wouldn't have it any other way, Vee trust me. That's what I love you for, your stubborn, wilful, pain-in-the-arse independence. I mean you're not going for long are you? Not as long as last time? We've spent time apart before and we've got through it and truth be, we probably will do again. So, go for it. I'll miss you, of course I'll miss you, I love you, you know that. But we're strong.'

'OK. OK. But...don't you want to know what I'll be doing over there?'

'Not really. I mean I know that you'll be taking photographs and doing good works. And I know that you'll take care of yourself. I mean you will won't you? You always do, right?'

'Ye-es,' said Vee, 'I suppose so...listen, Arch, I've just thought of something I've got to do tonight. Some work. For the trip. You don't mind if we don't tonight? Do you?'

I paused. For once I did. Partly because I had been looking forward to a night of Vee. Notwithstanding the good nature with which I had welcomed her news, I was jittery in the sweats. Since Wanstonia's tree had come down my life had consisted of nothing but violence and the simple honesty of techno. A bit of a spraff would have done me good, some comfort wine, a few ameliorative bifters. Some gags, the warming shadow of the affirmative. The big one was over and for all of her Very Fucking Drolls Vee wasn't about to jump out of a window or punch anyone's head or set fire to any newly consecrated squats...

And partly because I had a feeling that reminded me of what I'd felt when we'd first met. A feeling, from somewhere, of dread.

I said:
'No, not at all. Later, yeah? Sweetheart?'
and left.

The next night was clear and cold as the moon. Vee came round to the squat at seven and suggested we go for a walk. Her voice was tired. The air was freezing and my blood was thick in my veins. We walked down Salisbury Road to crawl into the private park through the hole in the fence. It was boarded-up.
'What do you want to do now?' I said.
She said 'We could go and sit outside the church on St Mary's Row.'
'Why?'
'Because it's quiet. There's something I want to tell you.'
'Again?'

'Again.'

Vee didn't say anything until we reached the churchyard. We climbed the steps, sat on a bench by moonstruck gravestones. I turned to look at her face. She turned away, suddenly, as if hiding something and in that moment, as my chest tightened and I shuddered to my core, I knew why she had brought me here.

'Jesus, Vee, what is it?' I said, barely able to form the words. 'It's not serious is it?'

'Yes,' she said and then she waited.

'I'm sorry Arch.'

'But. Why?'

'I'd always planned on seeing how things went. After I'd gone back to Croatia. You know, between us. But I don't think I can do it anymore, I just don't think I can.'

I stood up. Walked around in a figure of eight, stubbed my toe into a pebble, watched it fly over the wall that bordered the graveyard. It skipped across the frosty surface of the empty road below. I took a step to steady myself. Turned back to Vee.

'What do you mean?' I said.

'It was what you said about Tom,' she said. 'And what you said last night about the fire in your house. And then when I said I was going back...'

'I don't understand.'

'It's over Arch. I can't do it anymore.'

'But what is it Vee? Can you just tell me? *Please?*'

She stood up then. We were close to each other. She took a step back. I saw her suddenly exasperated maybe, or despairing. She threw her arms out, clutched the air.

'OK, OK, I'll tell you what it is. When I came back here you said you'd changed. Become more serious, if you like. It wasn't what I was looking for, but I thought I'd give you the benefit of the doubt, see how it went. But you haven't changed, not in the slightest. It's always about the easy option with you Arch, the easy answer to everything, answers that just fall from the sky after one too many inhalings or pills. Anything beyond the end of your nose and you're not interested. You weren't interested when I met you and you're not interested now. I've never known anyone as incurious as you. Not just you personally, all of you, and here, in Moseley, of all places. There's a complete lack of curiosity, a complete lack of, of a willingness to look at or engage, seriously, with the realities of other people, people not bound-up in spoiled *pissy* Western complacency.'

I nearly asked what this had to do with us but I wasn't about to give her that satisfaction. I took instead a deep lungful of godless air, and spluttered:
'Complacency? What are we doing that's complacent Vee? What the fuck's complacent about fighting for personal freedom? About demanding an alternative to this corporate bull shit-storm? About global ecology?'
'Oh yeah, I forgot about the whole saving the planet thing. In amongst all that stuff about your god-given right to party. So let me see, what's your take on it all? Oh yeah. Cars – bad, parties in tree-houses – good. Very constructive, I must say. Or is there something I've missed?'
'So now, at last, you've come out and said it. You've taken your time about it I must say. But then that's typical you, isn't it Vee? At least we're getting things done. At least we're bringing our beliefs to people's attention, stirring it up, getting in their faces. And if you're better than this, if you're the fucking Queen Stone,

then what, exactly, are you doing about what gets your goat? Whatever, exactly, that is?'

'*What gets my goat?* What gets my goat is that some people, people like you Arch, for Christ's sake, supposedly sussed, politically active educated people, people like Moseley, are so precious and cosseted and wrapped-up in themselves that they'll march for the right to party but need stirring-up about genocide. What gets my goat is that labour camps need to be shoved in people's faces and and that you seem to care more about being able to listen to techno than the fact that people are using rape, Arch, as a weapon of war, not three hours from here. *I mean you think you're what's coming next for fuck's sake!* You may be around here Arch but nowhere else, I'll tell you that.'

She paused. My face was hot. She tried to look me in the eye.

'Look. Arch. I think your politics are interesting, I do. And it's good that you're doing something, because this government is doing bad things. But that's not the point. I'm not talking about the rights and wrongs of what you're doing, I'm talking about where it's come from, what your politics say about us, our culture, our priorities. Our level of engagement with the world. About our idea of the truth about things, if you want to put it like that. In fact, yes, that should pretty much do it. Let's talk about your idea of the truth. Because anyone can make their own sense of the world, that's not difficult. Anyone can wallow in their personal experience and the personal experiences of people like them and then filter everything through what little they've learned in their wallowing. But the truth is about more than that. It's about more than the personal, the *parochial*. It's about going further, working harder. And the thing is, you haven't got the stomach for it any more, any of it, any of you. You can't deal with it. *You can't handle the truth,* Arch, that's from a film, how about that for irony? And you don't even want to try.

And do you know something? I've been letting it go, for both of our sakes. I mean I've tried, I have made the effort, I have tried. I've sat through your meetings, I've listened to your arguments. I've tried. But it's not enough and I can't be doing with it any more. Any of it.'

I threw my head back, gritted my teeth. How had this happened? It didn't seem possible. I knew I had been unfairly traduced and yet still I had nowhere to go.

'But Vee, I still don't understand. I feel the same way about you now as I've always done.'

'Bloody feelings! That's all there is these days! Feelings, sensation, personal hurt, personal fucking pain! Oh Arch, look, I'm sorry. I was happy when you said you loved me. I needed that, I really needed it. I don't know how I'd have got on without it. And I loved you, Arch, I did, really I did. But that just isn't enough, not any more. Try to understand, please try to understand.'

She wiped her face with her arm, rubbed her face with the palms of her hands. She was crying. The sound wasn't from around here. Now I was desperate. I wanted to take hold of her. Like a lover would take hold of someone he has spent the night loving. I wanted to reassure her. *Reassure me.* But I didn't know how to. We weren't those lovers any more. Were we ever?

I stood there. Wondered what I could do. There was nothing. It was already too late. It was already over.

'I've had enough of this,' I said, 'I want to go home,' and Vee didn't say anything to try and stop me as I left her under the church in the graveyard and walked, shivering, down the steps to the street.

~

By the time I got home I was sick to the bone and drained, of energies I didn't know I'd had or needed. I didn't want to think.

Sorrell was in the living room, on her own, drinking from a bottle of two quid Spanish wine. She was listening to Chumbawumba.

Fuck me.

Chumbawumba.

I said 'can I pinch a drink?' and she said 'yeah, go ahead. You OK?'
I sat next to her on the sofa. I said 'no, not really.'
She said, 'it's a shame Arch, me and you, yeah. Sometimes it seems we're the only people who don't take things too seriously. I think we could have, you know, maybe...'

She was right, of course. I'd been kidding myself when I'd told myself she was wrong. It would have been the opposite of opposites attracting. It would have saved a lot of trouble. She put her head on my chest and I didn't move away. We stayed that way until the bottle of wine had been drunk and then we went to our beds.

23. 'After what happened in May I hope things will change.'

For two months after that I survived on a diet of instant noodles and Special Brew. I felt the blurring of shock into anger into bitterness, disbelief to defiance to surrender, anger to sorrow to regret and then round and round again, in circles, tiny dizzying circles of malign emotional energy, now febrile now implacable the bitch I loved her.

Thank fuck for DIY. In the squat we were taking care of business. The landlord got in touch to say that we could expect legal action to evict us but he was very unconvincing and I don't think he knew what he was doing. We were busy with visitors, people passing through and stopping by, come to offer support and help decorate, keep the art fresh, the space fluid and dynamic. By now, all of us were enthused. Sorrell - who had decided to stay on in Mose after all - hooked-up with a Super Eight film-maker and volunteered her services as an extra in a short about the party on the common. Even Mike began to acquire a Moseley identity, a relationship to the Village that had the makings of a cult. I suppose there was no surprise there. He was as happy taking the piss out of himself as other people. And with Stripe out of the way, we were an inclusive bunch and tolerant too.

Ig meanwhile, confounded my fears and continued his hop-scraping all over the country, consolidating his position as the man with the organic plan. He brought us news of Leytonstonia, the next great republic and of an idea to squat the whole of Claremont Road, the last houses left standing on the route of the East London Bypass. We heard of the progress of the Summer of Fun, of the hundreds of thousands who'd be on the streets of the capital on Mayday and then in July, in the mass trespass coming together on Twyford. He told us of the beginning of a protest in the Cuerden Valley, Lancashire, on Solsbury Hill in Somerset.

Vee had called my politics precious but she was wrong, none of this was precious. The people were on the move. We would be 'vindicated by history'. There was nothing precious here. No, this was real and it was happening here and now, happening in these times when everything was supposed to have stopped, happening in this new year of 1994, when all of us involved knew that we could change things and more, when all of us felt that we could change the way that things are done.

~

As for the fire, it seemed that no-one else knew what had actually happened. I wondered how long it would be before Tom re-appeared and how much of his plan to prove his love for Sorrell he would share with her. It had been a strange plan, all things considered and I suspected he'd want to keep at least half of it to himself. After I began to appreciate what he'd done, I tried, briefly, to be angry with him. I failed. He'd gone too far, sure, but that was what he did. What had happened had happened. It had all seemed a bit unreal to tell the truth. And it had been a reassuringly pathetic effort. He had knocked the door, after all, rung the fire brigade, just to make sure.

It was effective though. I presumed that Tom would have made sure that his rival didn't have an alibi for his whereabouts at the time the fire started but then he knew the ways of the itinerant Moseley head better than most and was probably just hedging his unhinged bets. The coppers would know about Torpedo Town after all; that and hearsay would probably be all they'd needed to frame a rabble-rouser like Stripe, even one who'd roused no perceivable rabble.

They picked him up on the afternoon of the 4nd January. No-one saw him after that until he appeared in the Evening Mail, six months later, sent down for seven years for an attempted arson in Wolverhampton.

~

Wanstonia was evicted on February 16 1994. There were 700 old bill on site. It took 11 hours, cost the Department of Transport untold thousands. That same week, a bomb went off in Sarajevo market, killing 68 people. On the news they said that it was the worst atrocity in the conflict since a mortar landed on a bread queue in the city in May, 1992. At first the date didn't register but then I realised that Vee had made mention of this, at the time.

~

And then, as February's sometime borrowings dissolved into March morning mists and it seemed as though the whole world was shivering, I saw San in the Prince of Wales. Vee had left – two weeks, three weeks before? - and San asked me if I'd heard from her about how it was going, with Dejan.

With Dejan?

I was confused then bewildered. *With Dejan?* Yeah, people could run you over alright.

'Oh. She didn't tell you about Dejan?' said San. 'He's a friend of hers. Croatian. A photographer, from a village that was burned out...'

'And what? Were they...? Was she...? I mean were they...?'

'Oh no, nothing like that. At least, not seriously. But she was going to marry him, bring him over here. Get him out of there.'

'Really?' I said. 'She didn't mention it...'

'No. She said she was waiting for the right moment...I suppose it never came. She did say she was close to giving up...'

It was easier after that. I dragged myself brokenly home and accelerated through my processes like some kind of necessarily sick joke. At first all I could think of was betrayal. The way that she had used me, the way that I had allowed myself to be used.

Then I was pragmatic. What else was I supposed to do? What, exactly, could I have done? I'd risen to her challenge, after all. She'd told me I wasn't making an effort, so I had, I'd made my own sense of the world. I had my sense and she had hers and we had each other. Isn't that the way it works? Well isn't it?

The alternative was that I had given her too much space and I refused to believe *that*. Because this was Vee. There had always been pieces of her that were out of my reach, I knew that much, even as I convinced myself I didn't need to reach for them. That way lay over-complication, Tom, the doomed.

Lastly there was bitter relief. We'd had a strange relationship, a different, no, a *unique* relationship. We had experienced the great yes. Now she had nothing more to offer. There was nothing left to experience except a return to the banal expedient of walking through the fire distracted only by a relationship that was no different to anyone else's. And that wouldn't do for me.

Vee wouldn't have approved, of course, of the mechanisms I employed to blur her traces for a second time. They'd have been too simplistic for her. Not poetic enough. But if it was easier, if my answers were simpler than hers? So be it. I know now that I couldn't help it if she wanted more than this. She always wanted more. More than I had. More than I could give.

End.

It was San who told me what happened. Vee had been taking photographs in a village near the city of Travnik in the Lasva Valley, in Bosnia, the former Yugoslavia. She had been recording the activities of a Croatian army unit, The Jokers, who had operated there 12 months before. The area was quiet, peaceful. Almost serene? One day Vee left the house of the family she had been staying with and went off into the fields. She was looking for graves. She didn't come back.

They found her body a week later, under leaves. She had been shot. No-one knows who pulled the trigger.

What else can I say? Nothing more than I have already said. Nothing that would make any more sense out of what went on between us. There was a woman once and all that.

And there was.

And it might as well be all that matters. The personal pain. Because although she is gone, she's there in the stillness of the day. In the chatter too, alive even as it deadens my senses. However much she'd have had it any other way, she was with me in May when we marched and in July when we marched again, hundreds of thousands of us who shook the gates of Downing Street with techno and our righteous anger and with the energy from the party on Castlemorton Common. She is with me now, still, the loudest and softest part of the chatter, like the beat in my head. And every time I hear her I feel as though I have discovered the great yes all over again and then I feel an unbearable pain, to be buried again, because there is nothing else to discover and all there is, is loss.

Indigo Dreams Publishing
132, Hinckley Road
Stoney Stanton
Leicestershire
LE9 4LN
www.indigodreams.co.uk